"Why didn't somebody warn me?" Nash demanded

The smile had left his face and his voice was explosive. "How was I expected to know that Jake was short for Jacqueline?"

Shaken, Jake tried to make her tone light. "What's in a name?"

"In this case, plenty. In the first place, I've only had male trainees, and in the second—"

"I didn't realize that Australian men could be so chauvinistic," she said, interrupting him. "I'm as good a worker as any man, so there's no call to jump on me like a duck on a June bug."

"And in the second place—" he went on as if she hadn't spoken "—I'm not married."

The air she'd sucked in to continue her defence escaped in a rush. "Oh."

"Yes, oh. Now do you see the problem?"

Valerie Parv had a busy and successful career as a journalist and advertising copywriter before she began writing for Harlequin in 1982. She is an enthusiastic member of several Australian writers' organizations. Her many interests include her husband, her cat and the Australian environment. Her love of the land is a distinguishing feature in many of her books for Harlequin. Her home is in New South Wales.

A FAIR EXCHANGE

Valerie Parv

Harlequin Books

TORONTO • NEW YORK • LONDON
AMSTERDAM • PARIS • SYDNEY • HAMBURG
STOCKHOLM • ATHENS • TOKYO • MILAN
MADRID • WARSAW • BUDAPEST • AUCKLAND

For the wonderful people
at the International
Agricultural Exchange
Association—and
expecially for Anne, with
thanks for your inspiration

Original hardcover edition published in 1991
by Mills & Boon Limited

ISBN 0-373-17107-2

Harlequin Romance first edition April 1992

A FAIR EXCHANGE

CHAPTER ONE

SHOCK-waves eddied through Jacqueline's body. Bill Casey, crippled by a stroke? It couldn't be true. Kathryn Casey's haggard expression told her it was. Jacqueline reached for the other woman's hand. 'How bad is it?'

'Bad enough. It's affected his whole left side. He can talk a little but I can't understand most of it.' Her work-worn fingers clenched in Jacqueline's grasp. 'It's so frustrating for him.'

'Is there anything I can do?'

Kathryn shook her head. 'The doctors are doing all they can. Their main fear is of another, more massive stroke.' She pulled away and began to pace in a tight circle. 'I tried to get in touch with you but you were already on your way to Australia when it happened. I feel awful about leaving you in the lurch.'

'It isn't your fault. Bill needs you more than he needs an agricultural exchange trainee underfoot. I'm sure the Association will find me another host family in no time.'

Gratitude shone moistly in Kathryn's eyes. 'I called them as soon as I knew I couldn't honour our agreement. We've already got a new host family lined up for you.'

'That's wonderful.' But even as she reassured the other woman, dismay gripped Jacqueline. She had to live and work with this family for six months.

Would they get along? Come to that, were they even in the Riverina district? Her fingers curled into her palms so tightly that the nails bit into the soft tissue. After being so careful to match her agricultural interests with this area, it would be terrible if she ended up miles from here.

Australia was a big country even by Texan standards. If she was allocated to a farm miles from the Riverina, she might never find the answers she needed so desperately.

A man strode up to them and she dragged her thoughts back to the here and now. Kathryn hooked her arm around the man's waist and propelled him closer. 'Nash, I'd like to introduce Jacqueline McVey, the Agricultural Association trainee who was to stay with us before Bill's collapse. Jacqueline, this is our neighbour, Nash Campbell from Wirrinda Station, your new host.'

The man's eyes flickered from Jacqueline to Kathryn then back again, his gaze resting on her with disconcerting intensity. Feeling like a longhorn at a cattle sale, she extended her hand but he made no move to take it. A frown etched a V into his tanned forehead. 'Jacqueline? I thought your trainee's name was Jake.'

'My friends call me Jake,' Jacqueline explained. She looked meaningfully at her extended hand then let it drop to her side. 'Is there a problem, Mr Campbell?'

He started to say something, then glanced at Kathryn who was regarding them with ill-concealed anxiety. He shook his head. 'No problem. I'm sure we'll get along fine. Kathryn, why don't you get back to the hospital and Bill?'

The older woman forced a smile. 'If you're sure?'

He gave her a gentle push. 'I'm sure. Now get out of here.'

Kathryn enveloped Jacqueline in a quick hug. 'Thanks for being so understanding. I'm sorry about all of this. Call me when you get settled at Wirrinda.'

Choking on a lump which swelled in her throat, Jake returned the pressure. During the last few months she'd grown fond of the Casey family. Through their letters and photographs, she felt as if she knew them as well as her own family. This process ensured that the trainees felt at home with their host families. Now she would have to start again with total strangers. It was an effort to keep her distress out of her expression. 'Give my love to Bill and tell him I'll be in touch.'

Then Kathryn was gone and she was alone with Nash Campbell. The door had barely swung shut behind Kathryn when the smile drained from his face. 'Why in blazes didn't somebody warn me that Jake was short for Jacqueline?'

Shaken, she tried to make her tone light. 'What's in a name?'

'In this case, plenty. In the first place, I've only had male trainees at Wirrinda up to now, and in the second——'

'I didn't realise that Australian men could be so chauvinistic,' she interrupted him. 'I'm as good a worker as any man, indoors or out on the range. Back home in Texas, I've mended fences, branded cattle and spent fifteen-hour days in the saddle, so there's no call to jump on me like a duck on a June bug.'

'And in the second place,' he went on as if she hadn't spoken, 'I'm not married.'

The air she'd sucked in to continue her defence escaped in a rush. 'Oh.'

'Yes, oh. Now do you see the problem?'

'But you told Kathryn——'

'I told Kathryn what she needed to hear,' he cut in sharply. 'She was desperate to get back to Bill. It was no time to burden her with your problems.'

The way he allocated ownership of the problem didn't escape her. 'Surely there's a solution? I can't believe that you live alone on your ranch, Mr Campbell.'

'Station,' he corrected automatically. 'Out here we call them stations. And no, I don't live alone. My mother lives on the property, and there's also my sister.'

Jake's chin lifted defiantly as she strained to minimise the difference in height between them. But a tilted chin did little to make up for a six-inch variation in their heights. 'There, you see?'

'No, I don't. My mother is an invalid and, in any case, she's staying with friends at the moment. And my sister is a commercial pilot who only lives at home between charter flights. Neither of them qualifies as a chaperon.'

She could feel her chance slipping away with every word. 'Does the IAEA know about your mother and sister?' she asked.

He massaged his chin. 'You're not suggesting I should lie to the International Agricultural Exchange Association about my home situation just so they'll agree to let you stay with me?'

'Not exactly.' Somehow, she had to make him understand how important this was to her. Her expression became appealing. 'Mr Campbell, I've come a long way for this experience. If you turn me away, I may be placed on a ranch—I mean, a station—miles from the Riverina.'

'Why is this particular district so important to you?'

'Environmental agriculture is my specialty. Nobody else is as deeply involved in soil reclamation as you people are.'

'It's true enough, although we're trying to spread the word and show, by example, what can be done. But reclaiming eroded land and reducing the sediment loading in our rivers is hardly a popular cause. Bill Casey was—is—right at the forefront.'

'So are you. In his letters, Bill described the wonderful work you're doing along the waterways at Wirrinda.'

'You would have a problem finding a similar programme to study elsewhere,' he thought aloud.

She contained her surge of joy as she realised that she was winning. 'I would,' she agreed soberly.

'Very well, I'll see what I can do. But it's going to be by the book. I'm scheduled to lecture on the erosion problem during the orientation weekend, so I'll talk to the IAEA area representative. It's up to him whether they let you come to Wirrinda with me.'

As fast as they had begun to lift, her spirits plummeted. 'I know what the answer will be when you tell them you want a female trainee billeted with a single man.' The Association would never approve and they both knew it.

He looked thoughtful. 'It might not be as clear-cut as you think. My housekeeper left recently, to keep house for her widowed father. If I tell the area rep that I have a sick mother and no housekeeper, they may let you stay as an Agrimix trainee.'

'But I planned to work outdoors.' The Association's definition of an Agrimix trainee was one who spent half the time indoors on domestic chores, and the rest working outside. They were generally less skilled at farming than the outdoor workers and she resented being categorised this way.

'Take it or leave it,' he said easily.

Annoyance flared inside her but she checked it. 'I have no choice but to take it, do I, Mr Campbell?'

'None, if you want to stay at Wirrinda,' he said evenly. 'And call me Nash, Jake. We Aussies are an informal lot.'

Informal *and* inflexible, she feared. At least this one was. She studied him covertly. The tall, rangy Australian wasn't handsome in the conventional sense. He was much too rugged-looking, with a hawkish profile which was almost regal, as if he had been born to a position of authority and knew it.

His hair was thick and black and shone like gunmetal. A little too long, it curled over his collar and ears, softening his otherwise forbidding looks.

One thick eyebrow was slightly higher than the other, as if he was in the habit of raising it cynically. She shivered involuntarily. As her host and surrogate family for the next six months, he made Bill Casey seem like Santa Claus.

The eyebrow tilted now. 'Will you know me again when you see me?'

Flustered, she tugged at a curl of ash-blonde hair, pulling the strand into her mouth where she chewed it for a moment. It was Nash's turn to stare and she coloured under his inspection. 'Is something the matter?'

His eyes lost focus for a moment. 'The way you do that reminds me of someone. Are you sure we haven't met before?'

The North American trainees had only arrived at the Agricultural College for their orientation seminar yesterday, having flown into Melbourne two days before. Nash Campbell hadn't been among the officials welcoming them. If he had, she would have remembered. She let the hair drop. 'I don't think so.'

'At an environmental conference in the States, perhaps?'

'No chance. Look, I have to go get settled in.' His persistence was unnerving. What if she bore a family resemblance to someone he knew? She had taken the risk of being recognised when she'd decided to come here. But she hadn't expected it to happen so quickly.

He seemed puzzled by her brusque denial but accepted it. 'I'll see you at my lecture this afternoon.' He took her attendance for granted. All the trainees were expected to attend all the sessions which were part of the settling-in process.

She nodded. 'I'll see you later.'

As she turned to go to her room in the residential part of the Agricultural College, she could feel his eyes following her. Was he still wondering where they'd met before? The truth would astonish him if he knew. They could even be related, she realised, finding the thought surprisingly disturbing.

Catching sight of her mirror image at the end of the hall, she paused, studying it. What had Nash seen in her? There was nothing in her reflection which offered a clue. To her critical eye, she looked typically Texan from her sun-streaked blonde hair to her athletic figure and honey-coloured skin. A pair of cat-like topaz eyes appraised her thoughtfully. Maybe she was being unduly sensitive, mistaking healthy male appreciation for something more.

She was on her way to attend Nash's lecture that afternoon when she received a message that the Association had agreed to let her go to Wirrinda.

Despite his insistence on doing everything by the book, she wondered if Nash had mentioned his mother's temporary absence. If he had, she would never have been entrusted to his care. The small sin of omission made him seem more human, somehow.

In the classroom, however, any such notion was quickly dispelled. Nash Campbell, lecturer, was, if possible, more autocratic than before. He was also passionate about protecting the environment, Jake discovered to her cost.

'Perhaps Miss McVey will tell us how the problem of soil erosion is being addressed in southern Texas,' he said, catching her off guard.

With difficulty, she focused on him. Somehow he knew that she hadn't been paying attention and her skin began to heat under his searching gaze. Frantically, she tried to dredge from her memory details of the soil conservation programmes she'd studied in college, but his obvious impatience drove them from her mind. 'I'm sorry, I wasn't concentrating,' she confessed.

Nash gave a long-suffering sigh. 'Does anyone else have something to add from their local experiences?'

To her intense relief, the discussion swirled past her as the others compared notes. At any other time she would have joined in the discussion eagerly. Environmental issues had been her speciality at Texas A & M, the agricultural and mechanical college she'd attended. But Nash's recognition had troubled her. Could he possibly know who she was and where she came from?

He was looking her way again and she groaned aloud as he fired another question at her. 'Could you repeat that?' she asked, despair colouring her voice. She was going to live with him on sufferance for the next six months and she'd already given him the idea that she was a scatter-brained ninny. His 'why me?' expression was plainly readable.

'You *are* from the United States, aren't you?' he queried with exaggerated politeness.

She frowned. 'You know I am.'

'Then you should be proud of your country's record in reducing soil losses by almost five hundred million tonnes in the first two years of your conservation programme.'

Stung by his sarcastic tone, she felt moved to say, 'It was the greatest year-to-year reduction on record for any country.'

He lifted that damning eyebrow. 'Well, well, you *do* know something about the subject. I was beginning to think you were here under false pretences.'

Panic flared inside her until she told herself that he couldn't possibly have guessed the real reason why she was here. Or why staying in this particular part of Australia was so important to her.

Her birthplace—her home town—she corrected the thought painfully, was Corpus Christi, a city of a quarter of a million people, on the Gulf Coast of southern Texas.

For twenty-four years, she had believed she was born there. It was only nine months ago that she had found out she was wrong.

The lecture droned on as she let her thoughts drift. She would never forget the shock of finding out the truth.

Still aching with grief over the loss of her parents, Mamie and Lyndon McVey, she'd dreaded the need to go through their personal papers but had finally steeled herself to do it.

It was so hard to believe they were gone. They'd been on an errand of mercy, to bring back an eighty-year-old aunt of Mamie's who lived alone in the town of Victoria where a hurricane was expected to hit. Too terrified to leave and too frail to prepare for the onslaught, the old lady had telephoned her niece for help. Without hesitation, the McVeys had driven north to her aid. On the way home to their ranch, all three had died when the hurricane had veered off-course, smashing into the coast fifty miles south of where it should have struck.

Her parents were at peace now, buried in the family plot overlooking the range which Lyndon had tended since he inherited the land from his father. It was the only home Jake had ever known. Growing up there with her brother, John, two years younger but taller and broader by a yard, she had never doubted that she was Texas born and bred. Hearing 'Dixie' played brought tears to her eyes even now, and she had pledged allegiance to the American flag every morning of her school life.

It wasn't until she began sorting through her parents' papers that she discovered she should have been singing 'Waltzing Matilda' instead.

According to the yellowing papers she retrieved from her father's safe, she had been born at Seymour in the Riverina district of New South Wales. She was Australian by birth and the McVeys were her adoptive parents.

The truth was revealed in a fragment of a letter which had stuck to the other papers and been filed, apparently unnoticed until now. She stared at the Australian postmark in horrid fascination, barely able to absorb the message revealed in the spidery handwriting.

> To put your mind at rest, there is no way little Jacqueline Christine can discover her true background. Under our laws, adoptees have no access to their birth records so you may be sure she will always think of you as her real mother. And so you are in every way which matters. I have never seen anyone as destined for motherhood as you, my dear Mamie. God bless you. Alice.

Coldness crept over Jake as she stared, transfixed, at the letter. The more she stared at it, the more alien it appeared.

She heard John come into the office. One look at her rigid pose and white face brought him to his knees beside her. 'What is it, sis? What's the matter?'

Her throat tightened, locking the words inside. How could she tell him that she wasn't his sister at all? They weren't even related by blood. All her life she had been living a lie. It was as if her foundations had been swept away in the same storm which had claimed her parents.

Gently he prised the paper out of her fingers and read it in silence. Finally he released an explosive breath. 'Sweet heaven, this is about you?'

A statue would have possessed more life than she did. 'It says so, doesn't it?'

'But there could be another Jacqueline Christine, couldn't there? It might be a misunderstanding.'

In his voice she heard his yearning for reassurance but her forlorn gaze denied either of them any comfort. 'Look at the date on the letter.'

He did so and whistled softly. 'It's the year you were born.'

She turned an anguished face to him. 'Oh, Johnny, don't you see what this means? I'm not a McVey at all. I don't belong here, not really. I was born in Australia, into a family of strangers.'

At twenty-two, John McVey was a younger version of his father. He even sounded like Lyndon as he tried to take charge, although he must have been as bewildered by the discovery as Jake was. 'Even if you were adopted, it doesn't mean anything. This is your home and I'm still your brother. Surely nothing else matters?'

How she wished she could reassure him, and herself for that matter. But with the evidence in her hands, she couldn't deny reality. 'It shouldn't matter, but it does,' she said, her voice cracking a little. 'Who am I, Johnny? Who is little Jacqueline Christine and where does she come from?'

The question haunted her all through the emotionally draining process of settling their parents' affairs. She had known that the ranch was to come to herself and John equally and had made up her mind what she would do about it long before her father's lawyer confirmed the news. 'I don't intend to accept my share,' she said firmly. 'The McVey Ranch is your birthright, Johnny, not mine.'

'It's as much yours as it is mine,' he insisted, stunned by her decision. 'How do you know that I'm not adopted, too?'

'You only have to look in a mirror.' He was the spitting image of Lyndon McVey and there was no point denying it. 'Besides, the older hands still talk about the day you were born, how a hurricane was blowing in and Mom couldn't get to the hospital so you were born right here. It's funny, but it never occurred to me to wonder why nobody remembered the day I arrived.'

The discovery of her adoption explained many things, she realised now. The difficulty in getting any kind of official paperwork, the originals supposedly having been lost. And the lack of reminiscences about her birth in contrast to the stories surrounding John's arrival.

He regarded her worriedly. 'If you don't want your share of the ranch, what do you plan to do?'

'What I must. Go to Australia and try to find my real family.'

'Are you sure it's a good idea?'

She knew what he was trying to say: that they had given her up for adoption to people from another country, so they might not welcome her now. It was a risk she had to take. 'I'm sure.'

'And what then?' He wanted her to say she would come back and resume her role at the ranch. It hurt her to disappoint him, when she knew that he loved her as a sister. To her surprise, the discovery hadn't changed his feelings towards her and she was grateful. But she couldn't give him the reassurance he wanted.

'I don't know,' she said truthfully. 'It depends on what I find when I get to Australia.' She was glad he offered no further objections.

Starting her quest the next day, she found the adoption agencies kind but unhelpful. None of them could put her in touch with her birth family in another country.

The Australian authorities were even less encouraging. 'New South Wales law doesn't permit adoptees to have access to their birth records,' she was told. A few private agencies provided a link between adoptees and their birth parents but a lot of luck was involved. Both parties had to register with the agency and, once linked, had to agree to a meeting. The odds were against her.

John, bless him, had provided a solution. From a young Australian farmer who had been living with friends of John's, he learned about the agricultural exchange programme and excitedly suggested that Jake register for it.

'Normally, they only allow you to choose which country you go to, not the exact place,' John informed Jake. 'But if you have a particular agricultural interest, they send you to the part of the country where you can pursue it.'

'You mean if I'm interested in the kind of farming they do in the Riverina, they might send me there?' John nodded.

By the greatest good fortune, a lot of research into environmental issues centred on the Riverina region. Her studies in ranch management at Texas A & M qualified her to study this work so she didn't have to pretend an enthusiasm she didn't feel. She had been matched with Bill Casey, an authority on using salt-tolerant trees to reclaim saline soils.

At the thought of Bill, a pang shot through her. How the rugged bushman must hate being ill. Confining a man like him to a hospital room was like caging a wild animal. He belonged outdoors, not in bed, a prisoner in his own body.

What a wonderful host he would have made, she thought with a flash of self-pity, quickly suppressed. After the loss of her own father, Bill had filled a gap in her life. The thought that she could lose him, too, before they'd met face-to-face, racked her with pain.

He would have understood her driving need to come, she felt sure. Would Nash Campbell be so understanding? He didn't look as if he had a compassionate bone in his body.

'You haven't spent any time in Kenya, by any chance?'

She was jolted out of her reverie to find Nash looming over her. From this angle, he was even more impressive than before. The hawk-like profile was softened by a wide, sensuous mouth and miraculously even white teeth. His eyes were sea-green, she noted, seeing herself reflected in their gold-flecked depths. 'Excuse me?' she said, baffled by his question.

'I wondered if you'd been to Kenya recently,' he repeated. 'You seem to be afflicted by something very like sleeping sickness. Or is it my lecturing style which puts you into a trance?'

With a growing sense of dismay, she realised that the classroom had emptied around her while she was lost in her thoughts. She was alone with Nash Campbell, making his closeness even more unnerving. It was just as well that her host family included his mother and sister, she thought fleetingly. On his own, he looked as if he ate agricultural trainees for breakfast.

'Well?' he persisted.

'I wasn't asleep, I was thinking,' she defended herself. 'I'm really very interested in how you're handling the problem of soil erosion in Australia.'

'Really?' His dry tone mocked her. 'Since you gave Bill and Kathryn that impression, I trust I won't be disappointed now you've landed on my doorstep?'

His arrogance was unbelievable. He was her host, and a substitute at that, not her boss. Just because she hadn't hung on his every word, he had no call to be so high-handed. 'You won't be disappointed,' she assured him. 'My letters to Bill didn't misrepresent a thing.'

'I hope not. But I'll find out soon enough when we get to Wirrinda.'

She took a steadying breath. They had to work together for the next six months. It wouldn't do to make an enemy of him in the first few days, especially when she had no idea what help she might need in her quest. 'I'm sorry for creating a bad first impression. Can we start over?'

He folded his arms across his chest, his expression softening marginally. If he smiled, he would look quite attractive, she mused, then dismissed the idea. She wasn't here for that sort of involvement. Finding her roots was all that mattered. All the same, she found herself hoping that they wouldn't turn out to be related. For all his arrogance, he was quite a man.

He tugged at his chin, the gesture curiously appealing to Jake. 'I know you've had a rough time lately. Kathryn told me about your parents. Now there's this business with Bill. Are you sure you want to go through with the programme?'

Her topaz eyes flashed fire at him. 'Are you trying to say that you don't want me at Wirrinda?'

A hiss of annoyance whistled between his teeth. 'If I didn't, do you think I'd waste half an hour arguing with the area representative? He was all for finding you a new host family headed by a nice, safe married couple.'

Her anger evaporated and she sagged against the desk. 'You did that for me?'

'I don't like to see anyone get a raw deal.'

He would have done the same for anyone who had suffered through no fault of their own, but she had the feeling there was more to it somehow. Her heart began to race and she closed her eyes instinctively against the effect of those sea-green eyes regarding her so steadily. Unconsciously, she twirled a sun-streaked curl between her fingers then fed it into her mouth, stopping when his expression tightened.

'We *have* met before,' he said decisively. 'There's something about you which is so familiar. Your walk, your gestures...' He leaned over and twined a curl around his finger. It was a curiously intimate action and it took her breath away momentarily. 'This habit, for instance.'

'Lots of people chew their hair,' she said defensively. 'At least they do in Texas.'

'They do in Australia, too. My sister does it all the time.' There was the longest pause as he studied her face, feature by feature, as if searching for something. Her heart hammered in her chest. Then he shook his head. 'I can't pin it down yet. But I will. Just give me a little more time.'

CHAPTER TWO

THE assessing gleam in Nash's sea-green eyes made her feel like a specimen under a microscope. When he studied her so closely, was he seeing a resemblance to someone he knew? She caught her breath at the idea. Could he possibly know her birth mother?

The temptation to demand an answer was almost overwhelming but she remembered the promise she had made to herself before leaving Texas. Until she was sure of her welcome, she would keep her secret. She didn't intend to force herself on a mother who didn't want to meet her.

'Have you heard how Bill is doing?' she asked, to divert Nash's attention from herself.

A frown creased his forehead. 'I telephoned the hospital before the lecture. So far there's no sign of the second stroke they're worried about.'

Her breath hissed out in a sigh of relief. 'Thank goodness. I don't know how Kathryn would manage if anything happened to Bill.'

Nash smiled wryly. 'A clever deduction, considering it was based on your letters to the Caseys. But you're right, Kathryn and Bill are like two halves of a whole.'

'You sound as if you disapprove,' she observed, then wondered if she should have kept the thought to herself.

But there was no anger at her in his expression although his jaw firmed and his eyes narrowed. 'Another astute deduction. I disapprove of anyone giving up their individuality. You risk ending up as half a person.'

Who had led him to this conclusion, she wondered? In her letters, Kathryn had mentioned Nash, but mainly as their neighbour and Bill's partner in their environmental projects. His love life, if he had one, was a total mystery.

Not that it was any concern of hers, she told herself as she closed her notebook and collected her things. 'Will I see you at dinner tonight?' she asked Nash.

'It's International Night,' he reminded her. 'All the host families are invited. I was going in my capacity as a lecturer, so I'll be wearing two hats.'

His other hat being that of her host, she reasoned. 'I haven't thanked you for putting on the other hat,' she told him. 'It was generous of you, considering that you were expecting a male trainee.'

'Don't credit me with too much generosity. You may regret getting me instead of Bill Casey.'

'I was kind of looking on Bill as a substitute father,' she murmured, realising how wistful she sounded.

His mouth twisted into a wry grin. 'If you're looking for a father figure, you've picked the wrong man.'

It was out before she could stop herself. 'I wouldn't make that mistake.'

'Just as well.'

Some father figure, she fumed to herself as he left her. For a start, he was only a few years older than she was. Kathryn had written about attending his thirtieth birthday party, which wasn't long ago. And he possessed none of Bill Casey's paternal warmth which came through in his letters. No, there was nothing fatherly about Nash Campbell.

So why did he make her thoughts tear along like a hound dog chasing a possum? It must be the after-effect of losing her parents, then coming to a new country to have yet another change thrust upon her. Her feeling of confusion was probably nothing to do with Nash Campbell.

'Coming to get ready for supper?' Susan Rand, the other Texan in their group, pirouetted into the room, her shoulder-length blonde hair flying. Her eyes were bright with excitement.

Jake stood up. 'I'm ready. And it's dinner over here.'

Susan chuckled. 'There's so much to remember. Dinner instead of supper. Paddock instead of field. My favourite is "ute" instead of pick-up truck.' She prounounced it 'ewt' in the Australian way and grimaced. 'Will we ever qualify as dinkum Aussies?'

'I didn't know we were supposed to,' Jake commented. 'We're only here for six months.'

Susan shot her a conspiratorial look. 'You perhaps. I may decide to settle here. Haven't you noticed what hunks these Aussie men are? Take Nash Campbell for instance. Now there's a real longhorn man.'

A sharp sensation stabbed at Jake's mid-section and she sucked in her breath. Nothing Susan had said warranted such a reaction. The other woman was looking at her curiously so she forced a smile. 'It's early days to be making plans. We've only seen

Melbourne and the college. Who knows how we'll feel when we're with our host families?'

Susan gave an exaggerated sigh. 'You're right. But it's hard to imagine a more gorgeous man than Nash Campbell.' Her look flickered to Jake. 'I hear he's going to be your host.'

'The family I was supposed to stay with had to pull out.' She described Bill Casey's illness and Susan made sympathetic noises. 'Mr Campbell was kind enough to offer me a place,' she finished.

Susan rolled her eyes. 'Some people have all the luck.'

'Your host family might have a good-looking son.'

'Could be. Or I might visit with you on our days off.'

For some reason, Jake found the idea unappealing but couldn't very well admit it. She couldn't stop Susan from visiting Wirrinda if she chose to. The question of why on earth she should want to stop her preoccupied her all the way back to her room.

There was time before dinner to write a letter to Johnny at the ranch telling him about Bill's illness and her reassignment to Wirrinda. Not entirely sure why, she avoided mentioning that her host was a single man not much older than herself, saying only that she was staying with the Campbell family.

She didn't want John to worry, or, worse still, head for Australia with a shotgun. He might not be her brother by birth, but, if anything, he was even more protective towards her since the discovery of her adoption.

She also penned a note to Kathryn Casey, wishing Bill a speedy recovery and promising to contact them as soon as Bill was well enough.

With her letters entrusted to the college office for posting, she dressed for dinner. The last night of the orientation seminar was a special occasion for the trainees and their host families before they began their duties in earnest.

Telling herself that it was in honour of the occasion, Jake took special care with her appearance. Most of her work days would be spent in jeans and shirts, so it was a rare chance to enjoy dressing up.

Her choice was a shirred dress in black tricot with an inset of lace outlining the cleft between her breasts. It was a college prom dress, cherished as a gift from her father. The recollection of his proud reaction when she first wore it overcame any reservations that she might be over-dressed.

Winding her hair into a knot, she fastened it at the nape of her neck, frowning as several tendril curls sprang free. She would have to remember not to put them into her mouth. Her mother was always chiding her about the habit. *Used* to chide her, she thought, chilled to think that she never would again.

'Oh, Mom, I miss you so much,' she whispered at her reflection in the mirror. Her mother had loved Jake to dress up, complaining that she spent more time looking like a boy than a woman. And as for 'Jake': 'What kind of name is that for a lovely young woman?' Jake parroted into the mirror, smiling through the mist which clouded her vision. She couldn't change her nickname now, any more than she could change the fate which had brought her to Australia. But she could curb her hair-chewing habit which triggered a worrying response in Nash Campbell.

Nash was waiting for her in the dining-room. 'As I'm your host, you're at my table,' he said, pulling out a chair for her.

It was logical, but she found herself wishing for another dinner companion. She had the feeling that Nash didn't like her, although it wasn't fair to blame him entirely. He hadn't been expecting a female trainee and she'd made matters worse by day-dreaming through his lecture. It wasn't the best beginning. She decided to try to make amends during the dinner.

'How did you become involved in the exchange programme?' she asked after their first course of sliced melon was served.

'I was a trainee myself.' Seeing her quizzical look, he elaborated, 'Ten years ago, I spent seven months in the States and Canada, studying the farming of exotic animals. It's one of the reasons why I have deer at Wirrinda now, after developing the interest in America.'

'We have deer back home, too,' she contributed. 'They're mostly white-tail and German fallow deer. But the ranch's mainstay is Santa Gertrudis cattle.'

'I tried cattle but I decided the future is in deer,' he explained. 'I find chital the most attractive and prolific. Where most species of deer produce one fawn a year, chitals breed all year round.' He rested his chin on one hand. 'What kind of station work interests you most?'

She sensed the trap in his question. In Texas, the women in the family usually did the more genteel jobs such as bringing food to the field hands at dinnertime, or lunch, as they called it here. Or they might teach in a nearby town. It was considered faintly improper for a lady to work alongside the hands, although Jake preferred it to anything else.

'I do everything a man can do,' she said with a hint of challenge in her voice. 'About the only thing I'd rather not do is hunt.' This made her an oddity in her home state, but she hated to kill any living thing.

'That makes two of us,' he surprised her by saying. 'I'd rather stay up all night bringing a calf into the world than take life if it isn't absolutely necessary.'

Yes, she could see him holding the head of a pregnant cow, she thought. He would gentle it with his touch and reassure it with his voice, helping nature along with his own hands if need be. It was a curiously satisfying picture. Maybe they had something in common after all.

Between courses, she learned that Wirrinda comprised five thousand acres of cattle and deer country. It was considerably larger than the McVey Ranch, although both properties employed a similar number of people.

'Out here, most properties are run by families with only casual labour to help with shearing and lambing,' said Nash.

'If you're reminding me that I'll have to pull my weight, we were forewarned before we left home,' she said, wondering if the thought had been on his mind.

His green eyes slid from her face to the panel of lace through which the mounds of her breasts could be glimpsed. 'You don't look as if you have any weight to pull,' he remarked.

She was saved from the need to reply when the entertainment got underway. International Night was a tradition at these seminars, when trainees performed short sketches illustrating some aspect of their own country.

The Canadians did a send-up of the Calgary Stampede with trainees playing the cattle. It was a hilarious look at the world-famous rodeo, and by the end Jake was wiping tears of laughter from her eyes.

Throughout the show she was conscious of Nash's eyes on her, as if he was still trying to decide where he'd seen her before. Luckily, the memory continued to elude him, until by the evening's end she was sure he had given up.

'Did you enjoy the show?' she asked him.

'Very much. Considering none of you is a professional, you did very well.'

'Even the Statue of Liberty?' she couldn't resist asking. It was the non-speaking part she had chosen for herself when the American trainees were devising their contribution.

'Not bad,' he admitted. His eyes gleamed and she saw that he was teasing her. Then he relented. 'Your group gave the best performance.'

She felt a glow creep into her cheeks. 'Thanks. I'll never make an actress, but it was fun.'

'I got that impression, especially from the tall blonde who carried the American flag.'

'Susan Rand?'

'Is that her name?' He looked as if he would keep it in mind. 'Do you know her?'

'We went to college together. She signed up for the programme when I did,' Jake explained with an edge of annoyance in her voice. She told herself it was tiredness and jet lag. It couldn't be because Susan's attraction to Nash Campbell appeared to be mutual, could it?

She stood and stretched. 'I'd better turn in.'

He slid her chair back for her. 'Good idea. I want to get an early start tomorrow.'

'No problem. Back home, I'm always up early.' If he thought she would balk at his suggestion he was wrong. Rising early even on holidays was part and parcel of ranch life.

'Five-thirty it is, then. I'll walk you back to your residence.'

He was only being a gentleman, but she wished he would say goodnight at the door of the dining-room. Out in the moonlight, she was disturbingly conscious of his presence as they walked along the path towards the residential buildings.

Taking two steps to every long-legged stride of his, she wondered what it would be like to go out on a real date with him. Would he keep a swath of path between them as he was doing now, or would he match his stride to hers, dropping an arm around her shoulders to draw her closer?

Stop it, she ordered herself angrily. Maybe the Association was wise to insist that female trainees stayed with married couples. Then her imagination wouldn't be running riot like this.

A kind of magnetism drew her gaze to his hawk-like profile, dark against the moon-bright sky. He reminded her of the head of Caesar on a Roman coin her brother owned. Like the others, he had dressed up tonight and looked ruggedly handsome in a snowy white shirt and dark suit which fitted him to perfection. He looked more like a city businessman than the owner of a cattle station. A gentleman farmer, the phrase slipped into her mind. At the same time, some instinct warned her that he wouldn't always be a gentleman. She had the feeling that she shouldn't take anything for granted where Nash Campbell was concerned. His unpredictable nature was as dangerous as it was exciting.

A shiver of apprehension rippled through her and his arm slid protectively around her shoulders. 'You should have brought a wrap. The nights can be chilly out here.'

Then why did she feel a sudden sensation of warmth? She looked up uncertainly, surprising something unfathomable in his sea-green gaze, as if the warmth had reached him, too. For the merest moment, the bubble of heat isolated them, cocooning them in its aura. Then his gaze flickered away and he withdrew his arm. She felt rejected and it hurt. She hadn't invited the moment of closeness so he shouldn't blame his reactions on her.

She crossed her arms in front of her, the gesture defensive. 'Do the rest of your family know that Jake isn't a man's name?'

'They do now. Accommodating you posed a few problems but I've resolved it now.'

'I can bunk in with the other field hands. There's no need to go to any trouble,' she protested.

His glance was coolly speculative. 'I'm sure you could, but our jackaroos are mostly hot-headed young men in their teens and early twenties. Having you bunk in with them, as you rashly suggest, might cause some problems.'

'I suppose there are limits to this equality business.'

'Precisely why you'll be living in the main house.'

Her eyebrows rocketed upwards. 'With you?'

'Is it such a daunting prospect? I promise I have more control over myself than the average jackaroo.'

She felt herself colouring and was thankful that the moonlight provided some camouflage. 'I wasn't suggesting——'

'Then perhaps you should,' he cut in curtly. 'You might think you're one of the boys, but one day, some man is going to remind you that there's a beautiful woman under that cowboy exterior. I'd hate it to happen against your will, because you were too naïve to see it coming.'

Her breathing gathered speed and she controlled it with an effort. They were alone in the moonlight, the others having already said their goodnights. He stopped and turned, his mouth looming tantalisingly over hers. Was he going to kiss her now, to remind her that she wasn't one of the boys after all?

When she was certain he meant to kiss her, his index finger flickered across her parted lips in a travesty of a kiss. Disappointment welled inside her, turning to fury when his laughter mocked her. 'You wouldn't last five minutes in a bunkhouse full of jackaroos.'

Her eyes flashed answering fire. 'Of all the feudal, arrogant, opinionated...' She tailed off, aware of a sudden sensation of danger.

One dark eyebrow lifted slowly. 'Yes?'

'Maybe I should have let the Association find me another host family after all.'

'There's still time.'

A guarded look came into her eyes. 'So that's what all this is about. You're trying to provoke me into saying something unforgivable so you'll have an excuse to hand me over to someone else.'

He sighed, the sound of a soft whisper on the night air. 'You have to admit, it almost worked.'

'But why? My only crime is turning out to be female, and I can hardly help that.'

An ironic gleam lit his gaze as he looked down at her. 'Don't apologise for being what you are, Jake McVey. What you are is a beautiful, desirable young woman. And *that's* the real problem.'

A wave of heat engulfed her and she took a shallow breath. 'I'm not sure what you mean.' But she was only too sure, and she suspected that he knew it.

'I mean there's a very good reason why the Association normally places single females with married hosts. Anything else is playing with fire.'

'But you argued on my behalf. Why did you bother if you don't think you can handle it?'

His bladed hand slashed the air in a dismissive gesture. 'I have handled it. We've had jillaroos at Wirrinda before—female station hands,' he explained for her benefit.

'Then what's the difference?'

He smoothed his hair back impatiently. 'I wish to hell I knew.' In the silvery light, his eyes seemed deeper set, darker and more implacable. 'You're a mystery, Jake. I *know* we've met before and I've been racking my brain all evening without coming up with the answer.'

'Maybe there isn't one,' she tried, hearing the hope which coloured her voice. 'Maybe I remind you of someone.' Damn! Why had she added such a provocative thought, putting the idea in his head?

'It has occurred to me,' he agreed. 'But you're not *like* anybody. You're one of a kind. Special.'

Shivers travelled along her spine. What would it be like to be special to Nash Campbell? She was sure he hadn't meant it in any proprietorial way, but the image persisted until she drove it away. She wasn't likely to find out. 'Here's my building,' she said as a dark shape loomed before them. 'Thank you for walking me back.'

He stopped and thrust his hands into his pockets as if to keep them out of harm's way. 'Then I'll say goodnight.'

The air fairly vibrated between them, as if there was more to be said, yet neither knew what to say or how to say it. In his pockets, his hands were balled into fists, she noticed abstractedly. 'Yes, goodnight,' she said awkwardly and turned to go. As she did so, a strand of her hair caught in the zipper of her dress and pulled her head sharply back. With a gasp, she dropped her head back and thrust her hands under her hair, lifting the heavy curtain free of the zipper.

It was over in a second, but there was a cry of recognition from Nash. 'That movement. Damn it, I've seen Chris do that all her life. That's who you keep reminding me of—Chris!'

With her hand on the doorknob, she froze, a chill wending its way through her body. He was going to make the connection and there was nothing she could do about it. Why did it have to happen now, before she could visit Wirrinda and see the area where she was born? Now she never would.

'Who is Chris?' she asked dully, expecting him to name a woman friend or neighbour who might be her birth mother.

There was a long pause during which his breathing was amplified in the night stillness. 'Chris is my sister,' he said at last.

Then he didn't know her mother after all. It was just a stupid, futile coincidence. 'I see,' she said despairingly.

His hand clamped on to her shoulder and he spun her around so she had no choice but to meet his furious gaze. 'No, you don't see. You look like Chris because you're sisters. But you know it, don't you? It's the reason you're desperate to get to Wirrinda.'

'No!' Her harsh cry was too tragic to be an act and he was startled by her response. 'I didn't know anything about any Chris. I knew I had family here somewhere, but I thought when you looked at me you were seeing my birth mother. She's the one I came to Australia to find.'

'Well you've found more than you bargained for,' he said, his voice ragged with emotion. 'Because you and Chris are twins.'

Her vision blurred and dizziness threatened to engulf her. She rested her back against the rough brick wall, welcoming its coarseness to help her hold on to reality. 'I have a twin? Are we identical?'

'If you were I'd have spotted the resemblance right away. You're fraternal twins and you're as fair as Chris is dark. But so many things about you remind me of her. Your gestures and her gestures. That hair-chewing thing, and the way you tossed your head back just now. In this light, the resemblance is much stronger. I'm surprised it took me so long to work it out.'

Dropping her arms to her sides, she pressed her palms hard against the brick wall, letting the rough texture bite into the sensitive skin of her hands. The pain was like a harbinger of the pain she was sure he was about to inflict on her. 'Now you've worked it out, what will you do about it?'

'There's only one thing I can do. Send you back to Texas where you came from.'

Her head thrashed from side to side in feverish denial. 'No way. I came here to find my roots and I'll do it with or without your encouragement.'

He gripped her shoulders in a punishing hold. 'It isn't that simple. Chris doesn't know she's adopted. I only found out by accident when I was in my teens. My mother swore me to secrecy and I've kept that vow all these years.'

She ignored the pain of his hold and concentrated on convincing him of the justice of her quest. 'She has a right to know the truth.'

He surprised her by nodding tautly. 'I agree. But my mother is the only one with the right to tell her, and she won't do it.'

'She has to.'

'Why? Because you're selfish enough to want to find some new relatives to replace the ones you lost? My mother's health is fragile. It might kill her to have to go through this now.'

His jibe about why she was here hit home and she sagged in his grasp, so he was almost supporting her. 'I wouldn't do anything to hurt your mother or sister,' she said woodenly. 'But this means a great deal to me. I can't just give up and go home, especially now you tell me I have a twin. I must see her, even if she doesn't know who I am. Can't you understand how I feel?'

'I'm trying,' he said shortly. 'But it didn't take me long to work out who you are. How long do you think you could keep the truth from Chris?'

'You said she's away a lot of the time. I could work out in the fields whenever she's at home. We don't even have to meet.' At least not under Nash's eye, she thought with fierce determination. No man was going to keep her away now she knew that she had a twin.

'You would co-operate if I kept you apart?' His tone was frankly sceptical.

'Yes, I would.'

He released her and stepped back, his broad shoulders slumping. 'Not good enough. In your shoes, I'd find a way around any restrictions imposed on me. The risk is too great.'

Her chin lifted defiantly. 'Very well, go to Wirrinda without me. But you have no grounds to send me back to Texas. I'll get myself another host family and continue my search in my own time.'

His chest swelled as he sucked in a huge breath then let it out in an explosive sigh. 'You don't leave me much choice, do you? It would be better to have you where I can keep an eye on you, than to keep looking over my shoulder to see where you'll turn up next.'

'Then you'll let me go with you as planned?'

'Yes.' His hard gaze bored into her, dispelling her rising sense of triumph. 'But don't celebrate your victory just yet. There are conditions.'

'Such as?'

'You're to stay away from Chris as much as possible. If your paths cross, there's to be no hinting about who you are.'

Hurt, she crossed her arms over her chest and looked down at them. 'You don't give me much credit, do you? I wasn't planning to walk up to someone and say, "Hi, I'm your long-lost kin." Not until I'm sure of my welcome.'

'Then my conditions should be easy to meet,' he said levelly. 'My family is important to me. I won't allow you or anyone else to cause them distress.'

She gave a sigh of exasperation. 'I don't want to hurt anyone. I only want to find out who I am, then I'll go back to Texas where I came from. But at least I'll know the truth.'

He bent his head then lifted it, meeting her gaze head-on. 'This is important to you, isn't it?'

'More important than anything I've ever done before.'

His throaty chuckle was the first warm sound to pass between them in an age. 'I should have known,' he said huskily. 'Chris is every bit as single-minded about what she wants. When she gets a bee in her bonnet, nothing on earth can shift her from her course.'

His change of humour warmed her and her arms slid to her sides. She leaned closer. 'Am I really like her?'

'When it comes to stubbornness, you're definitely twins. I shan't know about the rest until I get to know you better.'

She had won! She was going to Wirrinda to find out more about her real family. Somewhere in the midst of her excitement, his words hit home. He intended to get to know her better. The idea filled her with a mixture of elation and longing, all intertwined. Until another thought cast a shadow over her pleasure. If she and Chris were twins, what was the relationship between Nash and her?

CHAPTER THREE

ONE, two, three, *thump*. One, two, three, *thump*. Jake was taking out her frustrations of the past two weeks on the harmless bread dough. But it was better than taking them out on Nash Campbell.

Not that she'd had a chance to take anything out on him, she thought, giving the dough another thump. After bringing her to Wirrinda and introducing her to the people who worked here, he had kept out of her way, assigning her to field work when he was at the homestead, and keeping her occupied indoors when he was working close to the homestead.

So far she hadn't learned any more about her birth family. Chris, her twin sister, hadn't been home since Jake had arrived, and Nash had refused to discuss the subject any further. Whether he didn't want to tell her or simply didn't know any more himself, she couldn't decide.

Well he wasn't going to thwart her so easily, she vowed, giving the dough a final whack. She planned to spend her free time in the nearby town of Seymour, going through whatever local records were available. One way or another, she would find her answers.

She piled the puffy dough into a bowl and set it aside to rise, covered by a damp tea towel. She had almost finished cleaning up the vast kitchen when there was a knock on the flyscreen door.

Jake smiled at the newcomer. 'Howdy, Jean. You're just in time for coffee.'

Jean's husband, Len Crawford, was the manager of the station. Jake had already taken a liking to Jean and her husband, which seemed to be mutual. Jean came into the kitchen now and sank on to a chair at the kitchen table. 'You shouldn't work so hard, Jake. Nobody expects you to be superwoman.'

One man did, but Jake kept the thought to herself. 'I guess because I'm here on sufferance, I feel bound to prove myself.'

Jean knew about Nash's reluctance to accept Jake as a trainee, although she would never know the whole story. 'I understand, but you've already shown how capable you are in the house and outside as well. Len was full of compliments after you spotted that leaking ball valve on the water trough in the north paddock. He was able to repair it before a lot of valuable water was lost.'

Jake coloured with embarrassment. She hadn't expected the manager to notice such a small achievement. 'Back home, it's a standing rule always to check a water supply point. I guess it's a hard habit to kick.'

'Thank goodness,' Jean said heartily. 'But I didn't come to tell you what a good job you're doing. You know that already. I brought you your mail.'

Jake accepted the letters Jean held out to her, elated to see a Texas postmark on one airmail letter. 'It's from my brother, John.'

'You miss him, don't you?'

'I miss him more than I thought I would,' Jake admitted. 'After Mom and Dad died, I thought there was nothing left in Corpus for me. I guess I was wrong.'

'Our roots go deeper than we imagine,' Jean observed sagely. 'I was born in England and came to Australia when I was six. I thought I was as Aussie as I could be, until Len took me to England on our twenty-fifth wedding anniversary. I was excited, of course, but I didn't expect to feel anything for England, having grown up in Australia.'

Jake lowered her letter. 'What happened when you got there?'

A smile tugged at Jean's mouth. 'The moment we landed at Heathrow, I realised I was home. This silly old fool burst into tears.'

Jake's look was full of sympathy as she finally understood her own emotional reaction upon landing at Melbourne airport. Just as England was Jean's home, Australia was Jake's and something deep inside her recognised it. Like Jean, Jake had grown up in another country which she loved. Yet the old ties remained unbroken, waiting to tug at her the moment she was within reach. It was an eerie feeling.

To shake it off, she made coffee for herself and Jean, putting home-made cookies—biscuits, they were called here—on to a plate in the centre of the table. Jean made a face as she took one. 'You'll have to stop baking all these goodies. I'm putting on pounds.'

'Nash likes them,' Jake said and earned a curious look from Jean. 'He's the boss, after all,' she added.

Jean glanced around. 'Where is the boss cocky today?'

'Out mustering. He'll be back for dinner if you want to see him. Then he's off again first thing tomorrow to show me a special project along Wirrinda Creek.' She had been looking forward to the expedition all week, although she avoided examining her reasons too closely.

The pleasure in her voice wasn't lost on Jean. 'You're quite keen on Nash, aren't you, Jake?'

'I admire the work he's doing to help the environment.'

Jean wasn't deceived. 'So his work is the reason why you light up like a Christmas tree every time I mention him.'

'You're imagining things,' Jake said. She liked Nash, of course, but she didn't know him well enough to react as Jean was describing. Besides, until she knew more about their true relationship, she dared not let her feelings get out of hand, something Jean didn't know.

Jean sighed. 'You aren't the first jillaroo to fall for him, I suppose.'

'I haven't fallen for him,' Jake insisted. 'I like him, that's all. But I did wonder why he hasn't married.'

Jean let the silence lengthen before she said, 'I hope I'm not talking out of turn, but I like you, Jake. I don't want you getting hurt, and, seeing the way you look at Nash, it seems possible unless I say something now. He has no intention of ever marrying.'

A cold sensation invaded Jake, although the coffee she sipped was steaming. 'Never? Why on earth not?'

'Did he tell you how his father died?' Jake shook her head. Nash had told her his father died when he was a teenager, but that was all.

'He was killed when his tractor rolled as he was working on the bank of a new dam. The downhill wheel dropped into a patch of soft ground and the whole machine went over.'

'How terrible.'

'It almost destroyed Nash's mother. She was devoted to her husband and, when he died, her reason went. It was years before she could function normally again. Even today, she's in poor health most of the time.'

'Nash told me she was an invalid.' No wonder he was so anxious to avoid upsetting her in any way, she added to herself.

Jean nodded. 'He loves his mother very much and has done all he could to keep her at home with him, although there were times when we thought she'd be better off in professional care. It's because of her that Nash hates the idea of marrying.'

'But surely any woman he married would care for her, too?' Jake commented, at a loss to understand the problem.

'That isn't why he keeps women at arm's length. He saw what love did to his mother. To him, the price is simply too high.'

It explained his reaction when they discussed the closeness between Bill and Kathryn Casey, Jake thought, remembering his disapproval when she mentioned it. His jibe about ending up as half a person now made sense. Having seen what happened to his mother, he was determined to avoid a similar fate. 'I see,' she murmured.

Jean's hand brushed hers. 'I hope so, for your own sake.' She stood up. 'Thanks for the coffee. I'll leave you to read your letters.'

The screen door slammed behind Jean but it was a long time before Jake bent her head to her mail. Her mind was too busy with thoughts of Nash. It was bad enough to lose his father so cruelly, without having to watch his mother's suffering as well. Having lost her own parents so recently, she knew only too well how painful it could be. Time would heal the wounds, but would she ever get over the aching sense of loss which thoughts of them provoked? Her heart went out to Nash for all he had suffered.

When she finally dragged her thoughts back to the present, she was still clutching John's letter and she opened it, immersing herself in the news from home.

John had never been much of a letter-writer but had made an effort for her sake, filling several pages with news of their friends and the ranch. By the time she had finished reading, laughter had replaced her sadness. Bless John for knowing what she needed to hear right now.

The other letter was from Kathryn Casey who reported that Bill was at home and out of danger for the time being. Her anxiety fairly quivered through the pages of the letter and Jake prayed that Bill would be all right. Thinking of Nash's mother, she feared for Kathryn's sanity if anything happened to Bill.

By the time she had finished reading, the bread dough had risen sufficiently to be kneaded again and she worked off her frustration on it.

Halfway through, she paused to wonder why Jean's revelation had made her so angry. It wasn't as if she wanted a relationship with Nash, so it didn't matter what he thought of love. All the same, as she watched the dough rise again after her pummelling, she wondered if the same thing could happen to a human spirit. Love should be an uplifting experience, not a crushing one. It was a pity someone couldn't convince Nash.

He was in no mood to be convinced of anything, she found when he collected her for their outing next morning. His mood was as black as the thunder clouds on the far horizon. She had already learned that rain seldom came of them, so she hoped Nash's mood would be the same.

He said little as they drove across the bumpy dirt roads which criss-crossed the property in a confusing network. She amused herself by finding which way was north by pointing the twelve of her watch at the sun.

'Do you know where you are?' Nash asked, noticing her action.

'North lies halfway between twelve and the hour hand. That way,' she said, pointing triumphantly.

'And at night?'

Closing her eyes, she recited, 'I find the long axis of the Southern Cross and extend it two and a half times its length. Where a perpendicular from that point meets the horizon is south.'

He mimed applause then returned his hands to the steering wheel. 'You've been doing your homework. It pays. Even experienced bushmen can get twisted in a fog or dust storm, or at night.'

'I told you I mean to learn all I can about Australian farming methods while I'm here. Didn't you believe me?'

His hands tightened on the wheel. 'When I discovered who you were, I didn't know what to think.'

'Is that why you've been avoiding me for the last two weeks?'

He swung the wheel hard around to avoid a ridge in the road then wrestled the vehicle back to the centre again before he answered. 'Is that what you think? That I've been staying away because of you?'

'What else am I to think? Whenever you're at the homestead you make sure I'm out on the property and vice versa.'

His gaze flickered to her and back to the road. 'Wasn't it what we agreed?'

'We agreed that I wouldn't make a nuisance of myself, not that you'd treat me like a leper,' she said.

His breath whistled out between clenched teeth. 'I'm sorry if you got the wrong impression. It wasn't my intention.'

She waited but he didn't say any more. Instead, he drove the vehicle into a paddock, waited while she jumped out and closed the gate behind them, then steered down the side of a steep embankment.

When he brought the car to a halt, they were at the rim of a crater-shaped excavation. It was surrounded by rolling hills clothed in green spring grass, reminding her of the foothills of California.

At the centre was a pock-marked gully ringed by ironbark trees. A creek meandered along the gully floor.

The beauty of the setting left her breathless. 'It looks like a set for a John Wayne movie.'

'Last century, this was a gold mining area,' he told her. 'They used to look for the ironbark trees which indicated quartz-laden gold.'

'Then those gullies are old diggings,' she interpreted.

'Correct. The miners cut down great quantities of timber to make their camps. Later the land was over-grazed and the rabbits moved in, destroying the ground cover which held the soil in place. As rainwater ran off the bare slopes, it cut these deep ravines and washed still more soil off the hillsides.'

She guessed where he was leading. 'Without the natural pumping action of the trees, the water table would rise and make the ground saline. Is that what happened here?'

He nodded. 'I wanted to put a dam in here but the area couldn't be used as a water catchment until the eroded land was reclaimed. A few years ago I started contour-ploughing the banks to control surface water, and seeded the land with perennial grasses to hold the soil in place. Thousands of trees have been put in which are slowly reclaiming those gullies. Later, I'll show you the weirs I've built to redirect the water.'

Her eyes shone as she caught his enthusiasm. 'It's a huge project but it shows what can be done.'

Her uninhibited response softened his harsh features. 'By reducing the rate at which silt is carried into the dam, I estimate I've lengthened its storage life by a thousand per cent.'

She began to scribble furiously in the notebook she carried with her at all times, wanting to capture every detail of the project for later study. Texas had its own erosion and salinity problems. What she learned here, John could put to good use at the McVey Ranch.

Nash's eyes rested on her as she wrote. Confusion was mirrored in hers when she looked up at him. 'What is it? What's the matter?'

'It isn't an act. You really care about this stuff, don't you?'

'It's important to all of us, to the future of the planet,' she said, feeling weak when she saw the intensity with which he was looking at her. There was an aura of almost missionary purpose about him which struck a chord deep inside her. At least in their concern for the environment they were at one. The warmth of this awareness flowed over her in a current she could almost feel. Unconsciously, she leaned towards him.

He had never looked more virile or handsome, she thought in breathless wonder. His muscular thighs strained his moleskin trousers and his khaki work shirt spilled open at the throat, exposing a V of dark hair which curled around the top button.

Her gaze shifted to his face which was in shadow under the wide brim of his bush hat. His eyes were hooded now as if he had shut them against something he saw in her. But what? Her chest rose and fell as she waited for him to say something to ease the strain between them.

When he did, he surprised her. 'I'm damned glad you turned out to be a woman, Jake McVey.'

Her breath caught in her throat. Even the native birds in the trees were momentarily silent, the bush sounds muted by the singing sound in her ears as she met his brilliant gaze. 'You are?'

'Too right I am. If you'd been male, I'd have a problem on my hands.'

Her body felt hot and cold by turns, the ringing in her ears almost deafening as she asked, 'And now?'

'Now, I can do something I've wanted to do since I first set eyes on you.'

She knew what it was when she caught sight of the purposeful glint in his eyes. When he moved closer and crushed her in a bear-hug of an embrace, his hands felt fiery through her thin work shirt. Instinctively, she knew that this was where she belonged. He held her so tightly that the buttons of her shirt bit into the soft flesh of her breasts which were crushed against the hard wall of his chest.

When his mouth took hers, a tidal wave of pleasure-pain engulfed her and her mouth moved against his in automatic response. She felt tingling waves of pleasure as his fingers played up and down her spine and she pressed closer, wanting his touch more than she had ever wanted anything before. He made a throaty sound which vibrated against her mouth, tantalising her until her tongue licked out to moisten her dry lips. As her flickering tongue touched the hard edge of his teeth, his hold tightened and his breath became a heatwave against her cheek.

An impish impulse assailed her and she asked teasingly, 'Do I still remind you of your sister?'

The sensuous movements which were slowly driving her out of her mind ceased with chilling suddenness. The muscles of his back became rigid under her fingers. When he stepped away from her, his mouth was set in an implacable line. The coldness in his eyes struck fear into her heart. What had she said to cause such a change in him? 'This is the very thing I dreaded,' he said in a hoarse whisper. She had the feeling that he was speaking as much to himself as to her.

Bewilderment made her feel light-headed. 'We weren't doing anything wrong.' For her, it had felt gloriously right.

Evidently not where he was concerned. 'There's everything wrong with it. I should have known better than to bring you here.'

Was the kiss a moment of weakness which he already regretted? Unhappily, she remembered Jean warning her that Nash wasn't prepared to get involved with any woman. He was a man with a man's desires but giving in to them apparently wasn't on his agenda. She masked her disappointment with a false smile. 'So we got carried away. It isn't the end of the world.'

'It won't happen again,' he said, retreating from her stiffly as if the movement caused him pain. He would make sure they weren't alone again, she interpreted his words. Disappointment flooded through her, making her want to curl up into a tight ball. She had welcomed his embrace with a yearning she hadn't fully recognised until it was satisfied. Having awakened her desire, he was now discarding it. 'Damn you, Nash Campbell,' she said in a fierce undertone.

His head snapped up. 'I can't blame you for being angry. We'd better start back.' He sounded cold and impersonal, a different man from the one who had kissed her. Yet she had reached some part of him, she knew she had. Now he was walling himself off again.

Nash drove back to the homestead with clinical precision, giving the task all his attention. She felt lonely, shut out. The taste of his mouth was still on her lips, and occasionally she slid her tongue along them as if she could recapture the salty tang of him. Her body ached as if with exertion but she recognised it as unfulfilled desire.

Without even trying he had made her want him with every fibre of her being, only to cast her up on the beach of his rejection like so much flotsam. She had never felt so lonely and confused.

'Have you made any more headway in the search for your family?' he asked, surprising her out of her dark reverie. His question was so unexpected that her body jerked against the seatbelt. She settled back, easing the belt away from her where it threatened to cut into the side of her neck.

'It's hardly thanks to you if I have,' she retorted. 'Apart from today, you've been the original invisible man.'

He slid a hand through his hair, the gesture weariness itself. 'I doubt if there's any more I could have told you anyway. I would if I could.'

She sensed that he was offering an olive branch, trying to make amends for his behaviour at the creek. 'You could start by telling me how you found out about Chris and me,' she said, deciding to meet him halfway.

He took a deep breath and flexed his fingers against the wheel, then relaxed them as he said, 'I found out by accident when I overheard my mother and father arguing about whether Mum should be writing to America. My father said the letters were dynamite. If Chris or you ever saw them, you'd know you were adopted.'

She inclined her head, remembering. 'I did see one of the letters. I found it in my parents' safe after they died.'

'What did it say?'

The shock of finding the letter had engraved it on her mind. 'It was only a fragment, there by mistake most likely. But it was postmarked Seymour, Australia, and gave away the fact that Mamie McVey wasn't my real mother.'

'Which is exactly what Dad feared would happen,' Nash said.

'Did they tell you who my real mother was?' Jake asked, her throat tightening on the question.

In the driving mirror, she saw his mouth harden into a grim line. 'Mum wouldn't say. She just swore me to secrecy, telling me that it would hurt Chris if she found out the truth. Chris and I have always been close. Naturally, I wouldn't do anything to hurt her so I gave my word.'

Jake half turned towards Nash. 'It seems strange that your mother insisted on keeping the adoption a secret. Isn't it supposed to be better for the child to know as soon as they're old enough to understand that they've been chosen?'

'When I thought it through, I realised the adoption must have been illegal. My mother must have been afraid that Chris would be taken away from her if the truth came out.'

'Surely it can't matter now?'

'Maybe not to you or Chris, but it could to my mother. If she did something illegal all those years ago, the shame of its coming out could be more than she could handle. For all I know, there could even be legal repercussions.'

Jake's hands fluttered like butterflies in the air in front of her. 'There must be something we can do?'

'Not as long as my mother is alive.' His tone brooked no argument.

There had to be a solution but there was little point in continuing the discussion while Nash was in this mood. She was sure he had only raised the question in the first place to make amends for his actions at the creek.

The memory of his touch was still vivid and she arched her back, recalling the warmth of his hands splayed across her spine. He had wanted to make love to her, she was sure, only stopping because he didn't want any involvement. It wasn't for her sake. He didn't care about her feelings, or he would be more helpful in her quest. He knew she didn't want to hurt anyone, least of all his mother. But she needed to know the truth about herself.

Jean Crawford was coming out of the homestead when they drove up. 'I've put a leg of lamb in the oven to roast for dinner,' she told Jake. 'I noticed you left some vegetables prepared so I put them on as well.'

'Thanks. I didn't expect to be away so long,' she said with a sideways glance at Nash.

He didn't react. 'We took a look at the Wirrinda catchment area,' he explained. 'The new growth is coming along well.'

If Jean sensed the undercurrent of tension between them, she ignored it. 'Len is happy with it,' she agreed. 'It's a shame more farmers don't start something similar before it's too late.'

Nash walked around to their side of the car. 'It all takes time,' he assured Jean. 'Were there any messages while I was away?'

'One from Kathryn Casey, letting us know that Bill is definitely on the mend,' she said. 'They're going to Bill's daughters on the Gold Coast for few days of rest and relaxation.'

'Do him the world of good,' Nash said. 'As long as he's at home, he'll want to be working if I know Bill.'

Jean nodded. 'Too right.'

Hearing them discuss their friends with such easy camaraderie, Jake felt like the proverbial fifth wheel. She started towards the house. 'I'll see to dinner.'

'It's a pity you didn't get back sooner,' Jean said in the same conversational tone. 'You'd have met Chris. She could only stay a couple of hours, but it was lovely to see her all the same.'

Her steps faltered and cold fury gripped Jake from head to toe. Chris had been here and she hadn't even known! She controlled her emotions enough to ask Nash, 'Did you know she was coming today?'

His quickly hooded gaze told its own story. 'It was only a possibility,' he admitted, tension vibrating in his voice.

'Now I see why you were so anxious to show me your precious catchment area,' she said dully. How could he have been so cruel?

Jean glanced uneasily from one to the other. 'Is something the matter?'

Nash patted her arm. 'Nothing that need worry you. You'd better get back to Len. He'll be looking for his tea about now.'

Still looking troubled, Jean headed towards the manager's cottage which stood in its own garden a short distance from the main house. When she was out of earshot, Jake whirled on Nash. 'That was a despicable thing to do, getting me out of the way because you knew Chris would be here.'

'I told you it was only a possibility. She might not have turned up at all.'

His calm reasonableness fuelled her sense of outrage. 'But she *did* come. Yet you didn't trust me to keep my word. You had to forcibly keep us apart. I can't believe anyone could be so inhuman.' Furiously, she scrubbed the back of her hand against her mouth. 'I'll bet you staged that little love scene down by the creek to keep me away from here for as long as possible.'

'What happened at the creek has nothing to do with this,' he flung back at her.

'Doesn't it? Next thing you'll be telling me it meant something, when it's obvious what you were up to.'

'Is it, Jake? I'm surprised such an idea would occur to you, you being so innocent of guile yourself.'

His barbed comment made her shudder. Was this his way of getting even with her for forcing herself on to him? Since he made no move to deny it, she concluded that it was. Her spirits dropped even further. His kiss had seemed so warm and genuine. The fires he had ignited inside her smouldered still. Finding that his passion was an act to keep her away from Wirrinda for as long as possible made her feel used. Desperately disappointed, she turned away from him, her shoulders drooping.

He caught her arm and spun her back to him. 'I'm truly sorry you didn't see Chris,' he said, 'but you must see that it's for the best.'

'The best for whom?' she shot back.

His frown deepened. 'I didn't engineer this, no matter what you think. I enjoyed showing you my work.'

His obvious sincerity dissipated some of her anger. 'I enjoyed seeing it, too,' she conceded, then added wistfully, 'but I still wish I'd been here when Chris arrived.'

There was a long silence as he turned something over in his mind. Finally, he said, 'Would it help to know that she's due home on Friday for the weekend?'

Her sadness lifted like a curtain. 'Really? I can meet her then?'

'You promised you wouldn't insist on a meeting.'

Damn him for holding her to their agreement! Her shoulders sagged. 'I know. But at least I can see what she looks like.'

He swept his bush hat off his head and raked stiff fingers through his hair, leaving trails which she was tempted to smooth away with her hands. With an effort, she kept them at her sides, wondering at the source of such a crazy impulse.

'I should hold you to your agreement,' he said and she caught her breath, then he added, 'but I won't. You can meet her but no hints, no tricks. As far as Chris is to know, you're simply the agricultural exchange girl from Texas.'

She let her breath out in a huge sigh and nodded her acceptance of his conditions. It was more than she had dared to hope for from him. Friday couldn't come quickly enough.

CHAPTER FOUR

JAKE felt like a little girl again, waiting for Christmas to arrive. The only difference between waiting for Christmas and for Chris's return was that the former had been marked by the opening of doors on an Advent calendar which Mamie McVey had placed on the back of the kitchen door every year. This time, there was no calendar to mark the passing days, only Jake's own impatience driving the hours forwards.

Luckily she had plenty of work to distract her. It was time to wean the last season's deer progeny and it was Jake's job to help Len with the work.

It was good to be back in the saddle and Jake enjoyed the routine of bringing the stock in, one paddock at a time, with the assistance of Len's sheepdog, Nipper.

By the end of the week most of the deer were in, so Jake didn't expect to be sent out to the paddocks when she reported to Len for her work assignment that morning.

'There's only one paddock remaining,' she protested. 'Surely you don't need me along?'

Len consulted his clipboard and frowned. 'I wouldn't have thought so but Nash specifically said you were to finish weaning the deer.'

'Oh, he did, did he? Where is our boss cocky this morning? I'd like to discuss this with him personally.' Jake had fallen into the habit of using the

Australian slang for the owner, but this time it was said with a derisory sneer. If he thought he could play the same trick on her twice in a row, he was in for a shock.

As Len told her, he was working on the station's computer system when she stormed in. He read the anger in her expression. 'Is something the matter?'

With a flourish, she swept her hat off her head and slammed it on to his desk, scattering papers. 'As you would say, too right there is. What do you mean, sending me out to the deer paddocks this morning? You know what day it is.'

'I don't recall you being rostered off today,' he said mildly, the corners of his mouth starting to twitch.

His humour fuelled her anger. 'It isn't my day off, as you well know. It's the day Chris is due and I intend to be here when she arrives.'

'And you will be.'

Recklessly, she hurtled on, anger closing her ears to his interruption. 'I'm not going to let you...' Finally, sense filtered through and her voice trailed off. 'What did you say?'

'I said you will be here. I never intended to keep you out in the paddocks all day. The last mob of twenty or thirty hinds won't take more than four hours to muster. Chris isn't due in until dinnertime. I thought the time would pass more quickly if you had something to do besides watching the clock.'

Resting both palms against his desk, she dropped her head so her hair curtained her chagrined expression. She had totally misjudged him. Far from scheming to keep her away from Chris, he had scheduled some activity to keep her from counting the hours. 'I'm sorry I got the wrong idea,' she said in a muffled tone which escaped from under her curtain of hair.

'It's becoming a habit where I'm concerned,' he said. 'You seem determined to think of me as an ogre who wants to keep you from your heart's desire.'

She swung her hair back over her shoulders in two tosses of her head. Her eyes glittered as they met his. 'I don't think you're an ogre, but you must admit, I had good reason to misinterpret your orders.'

'I didn't keep you away from Chris last time, either,' he stated emphatically. 'Damn it, Jake, you have to understand my position. If I let you have your way, innocent people will get hurt.'

She had already been hurt but he already knew that. She wanted to believe he hadn't lured her away from the homestead so she wouldn't meet Chris, but it was hard when he was so opposed to her quest. 'I do understand your position,' she said stiffly. 'Why won't you try to understand mine?'

He stood up, anger quivering in every line of his body. 'I thought I was doing so when I arranged your schedule for today. If this is the thanks I get, I won't waste my time in future.'

Clamping her palms over her ears, she shook her head. 'Please don't. I've already apologised for misjudging you. What more can I say?'

'You can give me credit for being human, for a start.'

Her hands slid down the sides of her face and she cradled her chin in them. 'I never seriously doubted it.'

'Even when you were hurling accusations at me?'

She clasped her hands together in an unconscious gesture of supplication. 'Today isn't the easiest day for me, you know.'

'It isn't for any of us. It's like sitting on top of an unexploded bomb.'

'And I'm the fuse that could set it off.'

'Something of the sort.' He came around the desk and perched on the edge, bracing one leg against the floor while the other swung free. 'Go out with Len today, Jake. You're so tense I can feel it from here.'

He was right. Inside, she felt tightly coiled, like an overwound clock spring. One more turn and everything would explode into a thousand tiny parts. She made a deliberate attempt to relax. 'I am on edge this morning. Forgive me?'

Suddenly the tension in the room increased but it was of quite a different sort. His smile caressed her gently. 'It's forgotten, Jake. We won't mention it again.'

Her pulse leapt alarmingly and her heart began to thud so loudly that it was surprising he didn't hear it. All the tension inside her spiralled to one point, deep in the pit of her stomach, and she recognised the sensation of arousal with amazement.

Nash hadn't moved, yet it was as if he had placed his hands on her, so sensitised was her skin. The prickling sensation spread through her like wildfire. She took a half-step towards him before she was aware of moving at all. 'Nash,' she said softly, licking her lips which suddenly felt arid.

He looked at her from under lowered lashes, the deepened colour of his tan showing that he was well aware of the charged atmosphere which had sprung up between them. His knuckles whitened as he gripped the edges of his desk. When he spoke, it was in a deep, rasping voice. 'Get out of here, Jake.'

'But I didn't——'

'For goodness' sake, go now.'

So she did, taking the long way around the office to avoid the slightest contact with him, as if a mere touch could snap the fragile control he was exerting over both of them. When she was outside the door, she let out a sighing breath and slumped against the wall.

She had heard of sexual chemisty but this was the first time she had experienced it in such overwhelming force. One word, one touch, was all it would have taken for her to fall into his arms. If Nash hadn't been strong enough to order her out of the room, she doubted whether she would have found the power to move of her own volition.

The only thing she didn't understand was why Nash was so determined to push her away. He felt what she felt, she was certain. But he refused to give in to it in the slightest. Why?

Even Jean's warning that Nash hated the idea of commitment because of what it had done to his mother didn't seem to justify his rejection. Maybe he didn't want her staying around in case she exposed some skeletons in his family cupboard. Whatever the reason, the encounter had left her quivering with nameless longings which throbbed through her like an electric current.

It wasn't fair, she thought bitterly. Here was a man she could love, maybe already did love a little. Yet he had rejected her before he even knew her properly.

It was a few more minutes before she felt composed enough to join Len and the other jackaroos for the ride out to the deer paddocks.

'Did you talk to the boss?' Len asked when she rode up to the group.

'Yes. He wants me to help with the last mob.'

He noticed the drooping mouth and grinned. 'Cheer up, Jake. It'll all be over soon.'

Which was exactly what she was afraid of, she realised as she rode slowly behind him. Her stay here *would* be over soon, then she would have to return to Texas leaving part of herself behind, the part that was rooted in Australian soil. If only Nash were more approachable. She needed to talk to someone about her background, yet there was no one else in whom she dared to confide.

It was just as well that the last mob of deer proved difficult to handle. Soon her hands were too full yarding them and splitting the fawns off from the hinds to worry about her problems. Once separated, the young deer were drenched for parasites, then weighed and tagged for identification.

This activity alone took a good four hours. Then Len told her to put the nursing hinds into a small paddock and let the fawns in six at a time, to find their mothers.

'Just seeing a hind and fawn together doesn't mean they are mother and child,' Len explained as they watched the pairing. 'A hind won't feed any fawn but her own,' he went on, 'so as soon as we see them drinking, we know they belong together.'

Once the pairs were matched up Jake was assigned to record their numbers to be keyed into the station's computer. Afterwards, they left the fawns in the pens to become familiar with people and farm activity. 'If they're domesticated at this age, they remain quiet and manageable all their lives,' Len informed her.

'Rather like human children,' she said, and his laughter showed his agreement.

Too dusty and unkempt by then to return to the homestead, she joined the men in their lunch-room. Most of them knew her now and they teased her good-naturedly as she collected her lunch and sat down at a vacant table.

'Mind if I join you?'

She looked up to find Nash standing beside her table, holding a laden tray. Before she could answer, he slid into the chair opposite her, his presence effectively ensuring that no one else would join them.

'Enjoy your morning?' he asked.

Sipping her cold milk provided a few moments' diversion before she had to answer and she stretched it further by blotting the white moustache off her upper lip. He watched her intently, his dark eyes following the movement of the napkin from her lips to the table. Her own breathing quickened in response. 'The time passed easily enough,' she admitted finally.

Some of the tension between them dissipated. He broke a roll in half and buttered it lavishly. 'So you admit I did you a favour?'

'I suppose so.'

The roll crumbled into fragments as he clenched his fingers. 'Damn it, Jake, why won't you admit that I did something good for you for a change?'

'For a change is right,' she mumbled around a mouthful of sandwich.

'Maybe I haven't been all sweetness and light since you got here. But I have good reason, you must admit.'

She knew how much he resented any kind of involvement, but she didn't want to put Jean in an awkward position by admitting how she found out. 'I'm sure you do,' she said evenly.

'You don't give an inch, do you?' he growled.

She kept her eyes on her tray. 'Sometimes it's safer not to.'

He gave an audible sigh. 'You could be right.'

They finished their meal in silence and she became aware that the others were studying them with mild curiosity. She gathered that it wasn't a common occurrence for the boss to eat with the men, except when they were out on a muster camp, which was much more democratic. Why had he chosen to do so today? She found it hard to believe it was for her sake.

So she was even more surprised when, the meal over, he stopped her at the door. 'Like to walk back with me?'

She glanced over her shoulder. 'I should check with Len.'

'He won't need you again today. I've arranged for one of the men to stable your horse.'

'Thank you.' Her look of surprise slid to him then to the ground, which felt less challenging. 'Why are you being so considerate all of a sudden?'

'It doesn't say much for my image, if such simple things surprise you,' he commented drily. 'I thought you might like to relax and freshen up before Chris arrives.'

'Two favours in one day?' she said, arching her eyebrows. 'Careful, this could get to be a habit.'

A frown slashed across his forehead. 'Will you cut it out before I regret my moment of weakness?'

She doubted whether Nash Campbell had known a moment of weakness in his life, but she bit back the comment. For whatever reason, he was trying to be nice to her. So why did it feel as if there would be a price to pay at the end of it?

A buzzing sound overhead drew their eyes upwards and Jake caught a glimpse of the sun flashing off metal. 'Chris?' she asked, turning sparkling eyes to Nash.

He nodded. 'She's coming in early.' His pace lengthened. 'I'll get one of the men to pick her up from the airstrip while you change.'

She didn't want Chris to see her for the first time in her dusty work clothes so she made herself slow down long enough to take a cool shower and change into clean jeans and a chequered shirt. As she fastened the buttons, her fingers shook and she took a deep breath. Chris mustn't see how edgy she was, or she was bound to be suspicious.

Taking a last look at herself in the full-length mirror in her bedroom, she grimaced. Despite wearing the hat that Nash insisted on, her skin was tanned to a deep *café au lait* colour and her hair had lightened to a streaky golden shade. She had lost a few pounds, too, which couldn't hurt. What would Chris think of her?

Her gait was unsteady as she walked down the corridor to where she could hear voices in the family room. There was a formal lounge and dining-room but everyone congregated in the big, informal room off the kitchen.

Nash was there now, his back propped against the fireplace and a foaming glass of beer in his hand. But Jake had eyes only for the young woman seated on the sofa opposite him, laughing at something Nash had just said.

Like Jake, she was twenty-four, although she looked about eighteen. Do I look that young? Jake found herself wondering. The other woman was slim with straight dark hair which swung around her shoulders in a glossy curtain. Her eyes were smoky grey and a *retroussé* nose added to her youthful appearance. She wore no make-up other than coral-coloured lipstick to shape a generous mouth which tilted up at the corners.

As Nash had forewarned her, Chris was as dark as Jake was fair. Also, Chris seemed to be a fraction shorter than Jake, although it was hard to tell while she was seated. So there was no strong physical resemblance. And yet, there was something so familiar about the way she held her head, laughed and moved, that Jake understood how Nash had recognised her so quickly. Would Chris do the same?

Jake had to resist the urge to flee before Chris saw her. She reminded herself that this was her fraternal twin, her own flesh and blood. Excitement began to bubble inside her, the feeling almost intoxicating. If she left without meeting Chris, she would never know a moment's peace again. She made an effort to steady her breathing as she crossed the room.

Hearing Jake's footsteps on the polished tallow-wood floorboards, Chris jumped up, waiting with ill-concealed impatience for Nash to make the introductions.

He stepped between them. 'Jake, this is my sister, Chris Campbell.' Did she imagine it or had he emphasised the 'my'? She gave a slight shake of her head, rejecting the idea. She might not be able to acknowledge Chris, but that didn't make them any less sisters. 'Chris, this is Jacqueline McVey, our Agrimix candidate from Brooks County, Texas,' Nash finished the introduction.

Mastering her nervousness, Jake offered the traditional Texan greeting, 'How're you doing, Chris?'

Chris grinned, accepting her out-stretched hand. 'The Aussie reply is, G'day to you, too.'

As their fingers touched, an almost electric sensation flowed through Jake. Even without Nash's assurance, she would have known that Chris was special to her. There was no sense of a first meeting. Rather, it was as if they had known each other always.

Did Chris sense it, too? Jake wished she could drop some hint, say something to cement the warmth which flowed so readily between them, but Nash hovered beside them like an avenging angel. Jake had to be content with making polite conversation. 'Nash tells me you're a professional pilot.'

'That's right. I fly all over the country, visiting the various properties, delivering mail and food, you name it.'

'Flying such an isolated route, you must be a mechanical genius.'

Chris's ready smile flashed between them. 'Not a chance. I can change a spark plug if I must, but that's about all. Luckily for me, servicing the plane is a mechanic's job.'

She seemed so youthfully feminine that Jake had a hard time imagining her man-handling heavy parcels at a station airstrip miles from anywhere. When she said so, Chris grinned. 'We wanted equality of the sexes, remember? Well, we pilots were among the first to achieve it.'

'Do you work for the Flying Doctor Service?' Jake asked, recalling what she'd read about Australia before she came here.

'It's a big part of my job. I fly doctors out to accident cases, and take the medical staff around on immunisation tours, stuff like that.'

Jake accepted the Coke that Nash handed to her, and sipped it thoughtfully. 'You make life on the ground seem tame.'

Chris grimaced. 'It is, to a born flyer like me.'

Nash nudged his sister's elbow. 'Tell her about Victor Victor.'

'Victor Victor is my pet Tiger Moth,' she explained to Jake, her eyes sparkling with enthusiasm. 'I take him on low-flying trips off the beaten track, looking for ancient Aboriginal sites and artefacts. Sometimes I do stunt flying for charity.' Her glance shifted to Nash. 'Big brother doesn't like me doing stunt work.'

He took a swallow of his beer and wiped the foam off his mouth with a crooked finger. 'Since when has my opinion made a difference?'

'Too true,' Chris agreed airily, then leaned towards Jake. 'Do you know what brothers are like?'

'Impossible, although mine is younger and more malleable,' Jake said, taking a slight liberty with the truth. She had about as much influence over John as Nash appeared to have over Chris. She savoured the moment of empathy, aware of Nash shifting from one foot to another. It was clear that he wanted this meeting over and done with. Jake wanted it to go on forever.

'How long are you staying at Wirrinda?' Chris asked her.

'Before Bill Casey became ill, I was to stay for six months. Now I'm not sure.' Her sidelong look at Nash registered his look of approval. At last she had said something right.

'With luck, you'll be here for my birthday party,' Chris pointed out. 'It would be the perfect chance for you to meet everyone in the district, wouldn't it, Nash? We could invite some of the other Agricultural Association trainees.'

Like Susan Rand. The name flashed into Jake's mind, provoking a strange feeling of resentment. The other Texan trainee hadn't yet visited Wirrinda but she had telephoned a couple of times and seemed to spend longer talking to Nash than Jake thought she needed to. She wasn't jealous of the other girl, was she? she wondered with a rush of chagrin. 'When is the party to be?' she asked.

'Two weeks from today.' She named the date.

'But that's my birthday, too.' Even as she said it, she didn't need Nash's thunderous look to know she'd made a mistake. But it was too late to retract it and Chris's expression glowed with excitement.

'That's terrific! We'll make it a double celebration, won't we, big brother?'

'If Jake is still here,' he said pointedly.

'Oh, come on, of course she will be. I've never heard of an Agrimix trainee coming and going in a month. You will be here, won't you, Jacqueline?'

'I guess so. And you can call me Jake. Everyone does.' She felt dazed by the speed with which Chris was taking charge.

'Then it's decided. I'll organise the guest list and you two can put your heads together on the catering.'

Jake felt as if she'd been hit by a truck. Sharing a birthday party with Chris was the last thing they needed. It was bound to draw attention to the similarities between them. It could even expose their true relationship. If only she had kept her mouth shut about her birthday, but she had blurted out the truth without thinking of the consequences.

Chris jumped to her feet. 'I'm pooped, but I still have to unload my plane. I brought you some of your favourite Redback Beer from Alice Springs,' she told Nash, then rolled her eyes at Jake. 'I'm strictly a champagne girl myself. In moderation, of course.'

'Me, too,' Jake agreed automatically.

Chris dug an elbow into Nash's side. 'Isn't this great? We share a birthday and have the same taste in booze. I'll bet we have heaps more in common.'

Far more than she knew, Jake thought uncomfortably. Maybe Nash was right, she shouldn't have insisted on this meeting. How long could she keep her identity a secret from someone with whom she shared so much?

'You couldn't resist it, could you?' Nash railed at her as soon as Chris was out of earshot. 'A joint birthday party! Why don't you simply advertise who you are?'

'You could have stepped in and vetoed the plan,' she retorted, hating to admit that he was right.

He thrust both hands through his hair in a gesture of frustration. 'As you may have noticed, when she gets an idea in her head, our Chris is unstoppable. Which is another thing you two have in common.'

Quarrelling about it wasn't going to help. 'I could pretend to be ill on the day of the party, or be working at one of the out-stations,' she suggested. Nash hadn't been averse to arranging it when it suited him, she recalled.

His jaw tightened and muscles worked in his throat. 'I'd catch hell from Chris and get no peace until I came to fetch you back.'

'Then I'll be ill that day.'

His heavy sigh rippled between them. 'Chris is perfectly capable of transferring the party to your bedside.'

She had run out of suggestions. 'Then it looks as if we'll have to go through with it.'

'There's another alternative,' he offered darkly.

Her suspicious glance met his hooded gaze. 'What is it?'

'You can go back where you belong.'

Oh, no, she hadn't come this far against all the odds to turn back now. 'You're forgetting that I belong here, too,' she reminded him.

'And, since I can't change that fact, the party goes ahead as planned,' he conceded. But there was no concession in the granite planes of his face. He looked grim as he added, 'And just to make sure nothing goes wrong, I shall be your date for the evening.'

'You mean my keeper, don't you?'

'Call it what you like. To our friends and neighbours, it will look as if we're in each other's company because we can't bear to be apart.'

'What if I refuse to play along?'

Half turned away from the window, his eyes were in shadow and looked deep-set and menacing. 'You will if you want to stay here another day. You may have been born here, but if Chris gets hurt because of you I'll make you wish you'd never been born at all. Is that clear?'

She executed a mock curtsy. 'Perfectly clear.' But inside she was seething. How could she have imagined she was attracted to him?

The unfairness of his treatment made her want to burst into tears. But, rather than give him the satisfaction, she pinned a smile on her lips as if she hadn't a care in the world.

CHAPTER FIVE

WHEN it came to throwing a party, Australian country people had a lot in common with Texans, Jake discovered. Nothing was too much trouble and there was far more food and drink than was needed.

She hummed to herself as she dressed. It was her birthday, too, and she wasn't going to let Nash's churlish attitude spoil it for her. Ever since Chris had suggested the joint party, he had been as moody as an approaching thunderstorm. It was likely to break over her head if she said one word out of place tonight. Not that she planned to, but it hurt to know that he was watching her every move while pretending to be an attentive escort.

The dress she planned to wear had been Chris's gift to her. Dismissing her protestations, the other woman had pulled it out of a duffel bag like a magician pulling scarves from a hat. 'I bought it in Darwin on my last trip to the Territory. The colour is wrong for me but it'll look stunning on you.'

Which it did, Jake had to admit, inspecting the effect in the full-length mirror. The dress was a simple chemise with wide shoulder-straps and a self-coloured frill draping fluidly below her bust. The crinkled crêpe de Chine was one of the most sensuous fabrics she had ever worn next to her skin and the jewelled colours showed off her Australian tan.

Her hair was coiled into a chignon at the nape of her neck, allowing only a few curls to escape. As well as making her look more sophisticated, it solved the problem of that darned hair-chewing habit. She'd noticed Chris doing it, and felt as if she was looking into a mirror which only reflected actions instead of your appearance.

There was a knock at her door and she went to answer it. At the sight of Nash standing there, something odd happened to her breathing, as if there was less air in the room suddenly.

In a charcoal double-breasted suit and pearl-grey shirt with a dark tie, he looked as if he owned the country. His thick black hair, still damp from his shower, curled intriguingly over his collar. It was a pity the softness didn't extend to his expression which was coldly assessing. 'Ready for pre-dinner drinks?'

'Just about. I'll get my purse.'

'You won't need a handbag tonight.'

'I have my instant camera in it. I want to take some pictures for my brother.' John had been asking for photographs since his first letter, but so far she hadn't taken any. Tonight was special. One of the guests she photographed could be her real mother. The possibility, remote though it was, sent prickles up her spine. Most of the district had been invited. Four-wheel-drive vehicles had been pulling up outside since early afternoon and several light planes had arrived at the airstrip while she was dressing. If her real mother still lived in the Riverina, it was just possible she could be here tonight. Would some sort of signal pass between them if they met? It seemed unlikely but Jake was alert for any sign. She slid the gold chain strap of her bag on to her shoulder. 'I'm ready.'

With his hand on the doorknob, Nash paused, looking at her as if seeing her properly for the first time. 'You look lovely, by the way.'

'Thank you.' Her prim tone was meant to convey that she hadn't forgiven him for his threat.

His frown said he got the message. 'Look, Jake,' he said awkwardly. 'I know I was against this party, but since it's a reality I propose a truce for tonight. I don't want Chris suspecting that anything's wrong between us.'

A shaft of disappointment speared her. The truce wasn't for her sake, only to avoid upsetting Chris. She was about to retort that she hadn't started the unpleasantness when she remembered that she had, by her very presence here. She had to shoulder at least some of the blame. And it would make a change not to be at war with Nash. 'It's a deal,' she said. 'Tonight, I'm Jake McVey, agricultural exchange person with no axe to grind.'

He looked relieved and held out a small gift-wrapped parcel. 'For you.'

'It wasn't necessary.' All the same, pleasure wreathed her features. She undid the wrappings to reveal a miniature gold-framed photograph of Chris. Her throat closed on her words of thanks.

He squeezed her hand. 'Don't say anything. I understand.'

She turned shining eyes to him. No gift had ever meant more to her. It was a piece of her roots, to cherish when she was thousands of miles away. 'Thank you,' she murmured huskily and reached up to kiss his cheek.

He looked embarrassed as he offered her his arm. 'Shall we join the party?'

Judging from the hubbub emanating from the living-rooms as they approached, the party was already in full swing. The formal living- and dining-rooms had been opened into one massive salon and it was thronged with people, most of them new to Jake. She tried to fix names and faces in her mind as Nash introduced her around, but she was soon at a loss.

One pair of faces was delightfully familiar, however. 'Kathryn,' Jake exclaimed, spotting her former hostess in the throng. The man beside Kathryn, although thin and pale, managed a warm smile.

'Jake McVey, you're even prettier than your photographs.'

She took Bill Casey's hands, noting how they trembled. 'It's so good to meet you at last. How're you doing?'

'I tire easily, which is annoying, but the paralysis has gone, thank goodness. I can talk again and be understood.'

'And he hasn't stopped since he came home from hospital,' Kathryn chimed in. But her pride and concern were very apparent and she kept a steadying arm linked through her husband's. 'How are you getting on with the Campbells?' she asked Jake.

'She's the very model of an agricultural exchange worker,' a voice answered for her. Nash moved closer, a glass of champagne in each hand, and gave one to Jake. 'You missed out on a hard worker, Kathryn. And a terrific cook.'

Jake could hardly believe her ears. The praise was mainly for Bill and Kathryn's sake, to save them worrying about her. But she hadn't guessed that Nash was so pleased with her work. The news warmed her.

'By your expression, Nash is being his usual miserly self when it comes to praise,' Kathryn said with a laugh then nudged Nash. 'Don't tell us, tell Jake how pleased you are.'

His mouth narrowed and his fingers tightened around the stem of his glass. 'Jake knows how I feel about her.'

Unfortunately she did, and some of her pleasure faded at the thought. She schooled her features into a pleasant mask and chatted to Kathryn and Bill without arousing their suspicions.

Apparently satisfied, they moved away and a pair of hands slid across Jake's eyes. 'Guess who?'

There was no mistaking that Texan twang. 'Susan, how're you doing?'

Susan released her and swung her around. 'I'm fine. Practically an Aussie by now.' Her eyelashes fluttered downwards. 'Aren't you going to introduce me to your host?'

'Susan Rand, this is Nash Campbell. Susan's from Galveston. We went to college together and travelled here in the same group.'

'Of course. You asked some pointed questions at my lecture,' he recalled, eliciting a pleased smile from Susan. 'You're staying with the Howards at Kookaburrah, aren't you?'

'My, you have quite a memory, considering how many trainees you must get through here,' Susan cooed, her attempt at an Aussie accent rapidly giving way to a coquettish Southern drawl. She hooked her arm through Nash's. 'My hosts are getting themselves some barbecue. I don't know a soul here besides you two.'

A savage sensation ripped through Jake and the stem of her wine glass bit into her fingers until she eased her grip on it. Nash meant nothing to her, so why did Susan's behaviour make her want to throw things? Jake hated Susan's studied helplessness which wasn't in the least genuine. During the orientation weekend, they had all seen her drive a combine harvester taller than a building, and throw a calf as expertly as any man.

Nash didn't seem to mind, Jake noticed, as their heads moved closer together. Susan was wearing evening pyjamas of some silky material which emphasised her feminine appeal. With a sense of shock, the Jacqueline inside Jake recognised that she was jealous. But why? She couldn't behave like Susan for anything. But it would be nice to have Nash's eyes soften when he looked at her, the way they did when he regarded Susan.

He threw back his head and laughed at Susan's words, and something tightened inside Jake. Her eyes misted as she turned away. She was probably homesick, that was all. Imagine mistaking it for jealousy!

'Cheer up, it's our birthday!'

Chris looked radiant in a black skirt and shimmering gold blouse, and Jake smiled at her. 'I can't forget it, thanks to your inspiration about the party.'

'And your catering. You must have worked for days to get all this yummy food together.' Her gesture encompassed the groaning buffet table and barbecue outside.

'I can't take all the credit. Jean Crawford and the stockmen's wives all helped.'

'Still, you did the organising. And you look sensational in that dress.'

In spite of herself, Jake's glance flew to Nash, but he was deep in conversation with Susan and several other people. 'I'm glad somebody noticed,' she said a little sourly.

'I've heard lots of compliments about our gorgeous house guest,' Chris assured her. 'But I know what you mean. My brother needs his eyesight examined.'

Alarms went off inside Jake. 'I wasn't referring to anyone in particular.'

'But I was.' Chris sighed. 'I despair of ever having a sister-in-law. I kept telling him you'd be ideal.'

Jake paled. 'Chris, you mustn't.' She didn't want Nash to think the idea was her own.

Chris closed her eye in a wink. 'Why shouldn't I speak out? I'd love to have you in the family. We're two of a kind, can't you sense it?'

The truth would rock Chris if she found out. She still had no inkling that, far from being potential sisters-in-law, they were already sisters by birth. Knowing how devastating the discovery would be to her, Jake had no trouble keeping her promise to Nash. But Chris's revelation filled her with sadness for what could never be. Jake couldn't stay where she was for another minute. 'I'm going out on to the veranda for some fresh air,' she said.

'Are you OK?'

'I'm fine. I'll be right back.'

But Chris insisted on following her out to the veranda where it was much quieter and cooler. Jake leaned against the wooden rail and stared up at the diamond-bright points of the Southern Cross. The stars were so clear out here, seeming close enough to reach up and touch. Yet the constellations were so different from home. A wave of homesickness swept through her.

'It's a beautiful night,' Chris observed, joining her at the railing.

She nodded. 'Australia is so beautiful.'

'But it isn't home.' Chris laid a hand on her arm. 'Is that what's troubling you, Jake?'

'Why should anything be troubling me?'

'I don't know. I sense a deep unhappiness in you, as if you have some big worry on your mind. You can tell me about it if you like. Flying alone around the outback, I've become a fantastic listener. Out there, I listen to myself for hours sometimes.'

Jake smiled weakly. What a relief it would be to unburden herself to Chris. Her understanding was almost a given. In a way, it *would* be like talking to herself. But for Chris's own sake she couldn't allow herself the luxury. 'You're probably right, I'm just homesick. It will pass.'

'You're sure?'

Jake smiled. 'I'm sure.'

'Sure of what?' A tall shadow momentarily blocked her view of the Southern Cross.

'Hi, big brother. Jake was telling me all her troubles.'

In the starlight, his eyes glinted ferally. 'What might her troubles be?'

'Homesickness,' Chris diagnosed. 'At least she assures me that's the problem. Maybe you can cheer her up. I have to go inside and circulate.'

As Chris went inside, Nash's relieved look followed her. Jake couldn't resist saying, 'What did you think I was telling her?'

His reply took her by surprise. 'I know exactly what you said to each other.'

Anger made her bristle. 'You were eavesdropping? Of all the low-down, despicable . . .' Her Texan drawl became more pronounced as she searched for something graphic to call him.

'Keep your voice down,' he urged, glancing back into the room.

But she was too incensed to comply. 'I don't give beans for what they think. I gave you my word I wouldn't tell Chris anything. You had no call to spy on me.'

Without warning, her words were muffled by the onslaught of his mouth against hers. His arms were like steel bands around her shoulders, moulding her against his lean, hard contours so that she was instantly, vibrantly aware of his maleness. Instinctively she tried to push him away, but it was like trying to move a mountain.

Just when his attempt to silence her changed into an embrace of mutual need, she wasn't sure. She only knew that in an instant the stars exploded into blinding brightness and the night became so hot that she felt feverish. Suddenly she didn't want to push him away. Her senses ran riot and she wanted him to go on kissing her for as long as this bewildering sensation lasted.

A low voice murmured words of endearment and it took her a moment to realise that the sounds came from her own throat. Nash's lips slid along her neck and across the ridge of her collarbone. Almost of their own accord, her arms linked behind the strong column of his neck, drawing him back to her mouth and deepening his kiss until she felt as if she was drowning in the sea of his embrace.

A discreet cough drew them apart. As sanity abruptly returned, Jake was glad that the night hid her blazing cheeks. What had she done, giving in to Nash like that? He had kissed her to silence her and she had not only allowed it, she had enjoyed it. What was worse, he knew the effect his kiss had produced. She wanted to shrivel up and disappear, but Len Crawford was hovering uncomfortably in the doorway.

'Yes, Len, what is it?' Nash's voice sounded deeper and more resonant than usual.

'Sorry to interrupt, boss. But those teenage hooligans are back at the chital paddock again.'

All Nash's attention was instantly on the other man. 'You did the right thing, letting me know. I want to catch them in the act.'

Still held in thrall by Nash's arousal, Jake forced herself to concentrate. 'What's going on?'

Len was the one who answered. 'A gang of teen-agers have been rustling deer. We think it's some kind of initiation for a gang but it has to be stopped.'

'And by heaven, it will be,' Nash vowed. He glanced towards the brightly lit room where the party was in full swing. 'Don't alarm anyone. Get two or three of the men and follow me down there.'

Jake didn't hesitate. 'I'm coming with you.'

'It's your party. You should stay here,' he argued.

'You don't want a fuss made,' she reminded him.

He correctly interpreted the threat behind her words. 'Very well, an extra pair of hands may be useful. But you're to do as you're told. I don't think there'll be much danger from a bunch of kids.'

Tempted to argue that she wasn't a hothouse flower to be cosseted and protected, like Susan Rand, she bit her tongue. Catching the intruders was more important than her feelings. 'I'll change and meet you out front,' she said.

Although he nodded agreement, there was no sign of him by the time she had changed into jeans and a shirt, although it took no more than five minutes. Breathless from rushing, she looked around the driveway, her frustration growing. Two of the station's four-wheel-drive vehicles were missing. Nash had gone off without her after all.

By pretending to agree, he had stopped her from making a fuss yet had got his own way in the end. 'Serve you right if I'd insisted on coming in my party dress,' she swore aloud.

Behind her, the music and chatter carried on the night air. Should she give in and rejoin them, as Nash obviously wanted her to do? He might need her, came a whisper of thought. What if the 'kids' turned out to be an organised gang, perhaps armed?

The memory of Nash's kiss was still imprinted on her mouth, recalling the hunger he had aroused in her. He might have kissed her to stop her from making a fuss, but her response had been a thing apart. For a brief moment in his arms, passion had ruled her. She had wanted his embrace, betraying her feelings with every ardent response.

Her hands twisted in front of her. Was she falling in love with Nash? If she was, it was the stupidest thing she'd done in her twenty-five years. She'd forced herself upon him when he didn't want her anywhere near his family. How could there be a place for her in his heart when he didn't want her in the same country?

None of that mattered now. Nash might need her help in coping with the teenage rustlers. She knew where the chital paddock was, having ridden there during daylight. But finding her way in the dark was another matter, even supposing she could handle an unfamiliar vehicle whose steering-wheel was on the wrong side.

Anything was better than waiting and worrying. In a flurry of activity, she located the remaining four-wheel-drive vehicle, hunted up its keys from the board behind Nash's office door and was soon on her way.

The headlights illuminated the hard-baked dirt road, throwing trees and fencing into jagged relief around her. It was a nightmare landscape, made more treacherous by the kangaroos which sprang into her path every few feet. During the day they slept under trees and in sandy hollows, but at night they appeared in astonishing numbers to bask on the sun-heated roads.

Dodging kangaroos gave her little time to worry about driving on what was, to her, the wrong side of the road. She had gone a dozen miles before she realised she was managing the vehicle successfully.

'I'll show you, Nash Campbell,' she said into her driving mirror.

Recalling Nash's warning that an experienced bushman could lose his way on these tracks at night, she peered intently ahead, anxious not to lose her bearings. 'Find the long axis of the Southern Cross,' she repeated to herself. Thankful that she had noticed the constellation earlier, she stopped long enough to calculate the point where a line extended from the Southern Cross to the horizon. That way was south. She was almost at the chital paddock.

The awareness slowed her to a crawl. Nash wanted to surprise the teenagers. He wouldn't thank her for barging in at full throttle.

Torches bobbed in the paddock ahead of her. Did they belong to Nash or to the rustlers? She decided to complete the distance on foot.

Although she tried to move stealthily, twigs rustled under her feet. There was a movement in the underbrush and a small animal scurried away. Where were Nash and the men?

A shriek of terror formed in her throat and was choked off by the pressure of a large hand over her mouth. Fighting the hold, she raked the air with her fingernails until they sank into yielding flesh.

'Ouch! You little...' The hand dropped away and she was pushed to the ground, sprawling on all fours.

'Nash?'

He dropped to the ground beside her. 'Jake? What the hell are you doing here? I thought you were one of the rustlers.'

She imitated his whispered tone. 'I had to come in case you needed me.'

'I needed you to stay put,' he growled. 'I can't look after you and chase the gang as well.'

His comment stung. 'I won't get in your way.'

'Quiet. Someone's at the fence.'

The sound of wire being snipped carried on the night air and she strained towards the sound, making out a dark shape crouched beside the eight-foot-high fence. The chital hinds were bunched into a corner and moved restlessly as the humans invaded their territory. If they weren't stopped soon, the intruders wouldn't have to harm the deer. The stress alone would make the deer barren for the next season.

The same thought was occurring to Nash, she realised, as she saw his body grow tense. For the first time she noticed the powerful spotlight clutched in his right hand. The intruder was already inside the paddock. 'What are we waiting for?' she whispered close to his ear.

'I'm waiting for Len's men to get into position,' he whispered back.

Adrenalin pumped through her veins. Rustling was as big a problem in Australia as it was in Texas. Rising prices for livestock and wool had led to the biggest outbreak of stock stealing since the nineteenth century. Even bales of wool and riding gear were targets. Stolen deer were particularly hard to trace because there was no branding or tattooing system in use.

This might be a teenage prank but Nash couldn't afford to ignore it, not with fawns fetching up to two thousand dollars each once they were weaned.

He eased upright and she copied the movement, waiting for his signal to move in. Her hand rested on the bag she had slung over her shoulder before leaving the homestead.

A commotion in the paddock brought Nash to his feet and into a sprint. He was almost at the torn fence before she realised he was moving. She sped after him, eased herself through the jagged opening and cursed as her bag caught on the wire. While she struggled frantically to free it, voices began shouting from all directions at once, and light beams criss-crossed the paddock. They caught a pair of kneeling figures with a chital hind thrashing on the ground between them.

'Watch it, they have knives,' Nash cautioned the others as he circled closer. Still hung up on the fence, she froze, her gaze fixed on the tableau. Like dancers, Len and his men moved in an arc opposite the rustlers. Nash was alone on this side, giving the knife blades a wide berth. Moonlight glinted on steel.

'Give me the knife, son. You don't want any more trouble.' Nash's voice soothed the rustlers as he might gentle a frightened animal. They were only boys, Jake saw with a sense of shock, as Nash's light played over them. They couldn't be more than thirteen or fourteen.

'You heard the man. We know this is a club thing. You weren't going to hurt the deer.' Len's tone matched Nash's.

The younger-looking of the pair glanced at his companion. 'Maybe we should give up.'

'Shut up. They'll have us for stock stealing,' the older one growled.

'No, we won't, not if you put the knives down now.' Nash took a step closer and the younger one dropped his knife. Nash scooped it up. 'Good lad. What about your mate?'

The blade trembled in the moonlight, as the boy wrestled with his conscience. He gestured as if about to hand the knife over, but when Nash bent to take it, another shadow loomed out of the bush behind him.

Jake put every ounce of power in her lungs into the scream. 'Nash, behind you!'

He spun, but not quickly enough to prevent the third man's arm from arcing downwards. She saw a flash of steel horrifically eclipsed by Nash's body. In shocked disbelief, Jake saw him stumble.

'No!' Her scream tore the air and she wrenched herself free from the fence. She was opening the bag as she covered the short distance between herself and Nash. A blinding flash turned night into day and the third rustler flung an arm across his eyes, the knife dropping from his fingers.

Len and his men closed in and the rustler ran. At Nash's shouted insistence, they took off after him.

Throwing the camera aside, Jake plunged to the ground beside Nash who lay with both hands clamped around his thigh. 'Nash, are you all right?'

'What the hell happened?'

'There was a third gang member keeping watch in the bushes. When he came at you with the knife, I blinded him with the flash from my instant camera.'

He gave a groan of appreciation intermingled with pain. 'What a time to take pictures.'

Relief flooded through her. If he could make jokes he couldn't be too badly injured. The breath she hadn't even known she was holding escaped with a rush. 'Thank goodness you're OK.'

'What about the gang?'

Car engines revved nearby. 'Len and the others went after them but I think they got away.'

'Damn. We had them red-handed, too.'

'You're forgetting,' she said, trying unsuccessfully to keep the pride out of her voice, 'I took their picture.'

'The hell you did. I thought it was just a diversion. You really have film in that thing?'

An anxious frown creased her forehead. 'Can it be used as evidence?'

'If it can't, it will give the police a good lead. They may have other evidence they can link with tonight's activity.'

His voice faded and she was immediately concerned. 'You *are* hurt. Let me see.'

'He caught me in the thigh. It's only a scratch.'

His scratch made her gasp in horror when she forced his hands away from the wound. His trousers were stained rust-red around a jagged tear. A ringing sound started in her ears and she shook her head. He needed her alert and functioning, not dizzy with shock.

'This will need stitches,' she said briskly. As she spoke she tugged her shirt out from her jeans and tore a strip off the tail.

The sound brought a tired smile to his face. 'This is just like a western film.'

Except that the blood was real and it belonged to a man she cared about, she thought grimly. Unlike the films, he wasn't about to get up and walk away when the director called 'cut'. If there was nerve damage, he wouldn't be walking for quite a while. 'Can you move your toes?' she asked, trying to mask her concern.

As soon as she secured the makeshift tourniquet around his thigh, he obliged her by moving each part of his leg. Only his sharp breath at each motion told her he was in pain. 'I told you it isn't serious,' he said irritably. She took his irritation as a sign that the pain was getting the better of him.

'So you keep telling me,' she said on a false note of good humour. 'If you're so brave, walking back to the car should be a snap.'

'Nothing to it,' he assured her, matching her tone. But he leaned heavily on her as they made their slow way back to the car. The arm he rested across her shoulders had saturated her shirt with his perspiration by the time she got him into the passenger seat.

'You're not going to pass out on me, are you?' she asked sharply. 'I want you to stay conscious until we get home.'

He faked an American accent. 'Yes ma'am. Whatever you say, ma'am.'

She gave an exasperated sigh. '*Now* you try to please me.'

'I thought I'd been doing that all evening,' he said in a low voice.

'That was for your benefit,' she flung at him, anxious to keep him talking until they reached the homestead. Despite her efforts to steer carefully, every bump in the road was emphasised by his indrawn breath. To distract him, she asked, 'Do you always kiss your staff into submission?'

'Only the ones I care about,' he murmured.

In the darkness, she stole a sideways glance at him. The pain must be making him delirious. Why else would he say such an extraordinary thing? 'Do you know where you are?' she tested him.

To her amazement, instead of answering, he started to sing. His voice was husky and strained, but still tuneful. The words brought a lump to her throat. Of all things, he was singing 'The Yellow Rose of Texas'.

Tears misted her gaze and she blinked them furiously away in order to keep the vehicle on the road. He couldn't possibly mean the words he was singing. He didn't think her eyes were as bright as diamonds, or that they sparkled like dew. And he certainly didn't care if they met again, that they never should be parted.

It was a bitter-sweet experience hearing a love song so dear to any Texan's heart sung by a man who meant so much to her, knowing that the words meant far more to her than to him. He was singing to keep himself alert and to fight off the pain of his injury, she told herself over and over again. But by the time the lights of the homestead came into sight, she was singing along with him and fighting to hold back her tears.

CHAPTER SIX

As soon as Jake brought the car to a halt outside the homestead, Len wrenched open the passenger door. 'Is he OK?'

Nash opened his eyes and gave a wry smile. 'You can address me in person. I'm still among the living.'

Len's craggy face creased in a smile. 'Saints be praised! When you went down, I wasn't sure what to think. But just in case, I asked Col Galen to stand by inside. It's just as well you invited him to the party but he made some cracks about people who want their money's worth.'

From this, she concluded that Col Galen was a doctor. There was a groan of annoyance from Nash. 'I don't want any fuss from you or Col.'

Joining them outside the car, Jake clucked her tongue. 'You should have thought of that before you decided to play the hero.' Her concern was reflected in her voice. Twice during the journey she had stopped to ease the tourniquet and on each occasion fresh blood had spurted from the gash. The sooner Nash was seen by a doctor, the better for her shattered nerves.

When she moved to help Nash out of the car, he waved her aside. 'In a minute. Did you catch those young hooligans?'

Ignoring Jake's restlessness, Len shrugged. 'Sorry, boss. They had one of those souped-up trucks that can outrun anything. But I managed to get most of the licence number.'

'Added to Jake's photo, we should have enough evidence to nab them,' Nash said.

Len regarded her with admiration. 'I thought I saw a flash go off. You kept your head long enough to take their picture?'

'It wasn't as calculated as Nash makes it sound. I took my camera along in case it should come in handy.'

'And it did,' Nash agreed. 'If you hadn't blinded that young thug with the flash, I might not be sitting here now.'

The very real possibility made her go icy from head to foot. She gripped the edge of the car door. 'Speaking of which, will you *please* go inside and get that leg attended to?'

Her desperation finally communicated itself to him. 'Yes, ma'am. But you should have Dr Galen check you over, too. You may have trouble sleeping tonight when the shock catches up with you.'

If anything haunted her dreams it would be the horror of seeing Nash injured, she thought, but merely nodded weary agreement and stepped aside to let Len help Nash into his office where Dr Galen had set up a temporary surgery.

Since there was nothing she could do while Nash was treated, she decided to wash and change. Her clothes were a tangled mess of dust, twigs and caked streaks of blood. The sight of it brought on a wave of nausea. If she hadn't thought to take her camera along, it might have been Nash's life-blood.

'Stop it,' she told herself. He wasn't seriously hurt so there was no point in tormenting herself with what might have happened. It hadn't and she should be giving thanks for it.

Chris came into the room while she was changing back into her party dress. It was hard to believe that less than two hours had passed since the adventure began, and the party was still going on in the living-room. 'Are you all right?' Chris asked. 'You're as white as a ghost.'

'I'm fine. Did Len tell you about Nash?'

The other girl's teeth bit down on her lower lip. 'He had to tell me why he wanted Col Galen. But no one else knows. Len said Nash gave specific orders.'

Jake tugged the straps of her dress into place. 'How did you manage to explain our absence?'

Chris stepped forward to close the zipper for her. 'I told them Nash had taken you off to show you the Southern Cross.'

Jake looked horrified. 'Chris, you didn't? Now everyone will think——'

'Exactly what I meant them to think,' Chris finished for her. 'With luck the rumour will get back to Nash and put some ideas into his head.'

'Ideas he won't welcome,' Jake said tiredly.

'You know how he feels about relationships?'

Jake nodded. 'Jean Crawford told me about your mother.'

'Then you know why he's so resistant to any kind of involvement. Mum took Dad's death awfully hard. She didn't want to go on living without him. But it doesn't have to be the same for every couple. Two people can have a close relationship without sacrificing their own identity. It was our mother's choice to do so.'

'But you've never married,' Jake pointed out.

Chris grinned.

'Yet.'

Her glow of pleasure was so evident that sparks of jealousy leapt inside Jake. 'Is there someone special?'

'He's a doctor with the Royal Flying Doctor Service. We started dating after we did a few immunisation runs together. Someone forgot to immunise me against him.'

'You don't sound as if you mind.'

'I don't. Unlike my dear brother, I want to be close to someone. Can I tell you a secret?' Jake nodded, intrigued. 'I've never told anyone this, least of all Nash. But I've always felt a bit of an odd one out in our family. Not that I wasn't loved and cherished,' she added hastily. 'But I'm so different from Nash and my parents. When I was a kid I fantasised that I was a changeling.'

Jake couldn't think what to say. As a child, she had also felt different, but had assumed that all children felt the same at times. 'I know what you mean,' she thought aloud.

'Somehow, I knew you'd understand. You're so easy to talk to, Jake. Maybe it was growing up with only a brother, but I've never had a sister I could share these feelings with. I couldn't tell my mother. She would be horrified to think I felt in any way different.'

A deep uneasiness pervaded Jake. They shouldn't be having this conversation. Almost anything she could think to say brought her to the brink of breaking her promise to Nash. She stood up and smoothed her dress down. 'Shouldn't we get back to the party?'

'You're right. I shouldn't burden you with my crazy notions.' There was a brittleness in Chris's voice which suggested that Jake's dismissal had hurt her. It was probably the first time she had shared these thoughts with anyone. Now it would be a long time before she risked such intimacy again.

Chris might believe that she was immune to Nash's fear of involvement but it was there all the same. From her mother she had learned that intimacy carried a risk. Jake's response had probably reinforced it. She wished there had been a kinder way to end the conversation but couldn't think of one.

'Where have you-all been? We're waiting to cut the birthday cake,' Susan Rand said when Jake and Chris rejoined the party.

Jake looked around. 'What about Nash?'

'What about him?'

At the sound of his voice her heart did a somersault in her chest and she spun around. He came in behind her, resting his weight on an ornately carved walking stick. He had exchanged the torn, blood-stained trousers for a new pair and he looked pale, but still attractive, framed in the doorway.

'Should you be walking around?' she asked, fear twisting like a knife inside her as she remembered the cruel gash which his trousers concealed.

'Probably not, but I don't intend to miss what's left of the party. There's plenty of time to rest afterwards.'

When he no longer needed to keep an eye on her, she realised. Even now he didn't trust her enough to leave her unsupervised. The doctor must have given him pain-killers to see him through the evening. 'I see,' she said stiffly.

His intense gaze speared her. 'Do you? I wonder.'

Susan waltzed over to them and tut-tutted at the sight of Nash's walking stick. 'What happened to you?'

Over the other girl's head, his eyes met Jake's, his look daring her to contradict anything he said. 'I was walking in the moonlight and didn't watch where I was putting my feet.'

Susan pouted prettily. 'I heard about your walk in the moonlight. Maybe you should take me along next time. I'll take much better care of you.'

'Oh, I was in good hands,' he assured her, earning Susan's look of disapproval. He was saved from further explanations by the arrival of a huge birthday cake resplendent with glowing candles.

Jake read the decorative lettering on top. It said 'Happy Birthday to Chris and Jake.' 'Was this your idea?' she asked Nash.

He feigned innocence. 'Who, me?'

'Who else? Jean was supposed to make the cake for Chris, not for me.'

'Now it's for both of you. Aren't you going to help Chris blow out the candles and make a wish?'

She needed two wishes, she found when the moment came. One was that she should find her real mother. The other, she hardly dared to whisper even to herself because it was so novel. She seemed to be tempting fate even thinking about it. She wanted Nash Campbell to love her, she discovered with a feeling akin to awe. Somewhere between arguing with him and saving his life, she had fallen in love with him. But it would take more than the power of a birthday wish to make him feel the same way.

The cake-cutting ceremony signalled the end of the party for those guests who weren't staying overnight at the homestead. Jake helped Chris with the farewells, feeling overwhelmed by the generosity she'd been shown. Although most of the guests hardly knew her, many of them had brought gifts and good wishes. When the Galens came to say goodnight, Jake shook the doctor's hand. 'How is Nash, really?' she asked in an undertone.

The doctor glanced over his shoulder. His wife was chatting to Chris. 'It was a deep cut and needed stitches, but there's no nerve damage so it should heal well if he gives it a chance.'

'Coming back to the party wasn't your idea?'

'Hardly, but you know Nash.' He leaned closer. 'I'm relying on you to see that he stays off that leg for at least a week.'

'Me?' she choked. 'I don't have an ounce of influence over Nash.'

The doctor winked at her. 'I got a different impression when I was stitching him up.'

'It must have been the pain talking,' she said, feeling her colour rise.

'All the same, he's well aware that it was your quick thinking which saved him from more serious injury.'

Pleasure spiralled through her. The doctor didn't know it but he had just given her a birthday gift more precious than any she had received today. 'I only did what anyone would have done in the same situation,' she demurred.

'Maybe, but you were there and he has a lot to thank you for.'

Knowing that he should be grateful to her wouldn't help their relationship a bit, she reflected. 'All we can do is try to make him follow your orders,' she told the doctor.

His laugh was sardonic. 'There's a first time for everything, I suppose.' Then he regarded her more keenly. 'But if anyone can influence him, it will be you.'

He was putting too much store by what Nash had said while he was in pain, but there was no point discussing it any further. The next few days would prove her right.

First there was the night to get through. 'Put those dishes down. Let the maids earn their keep,' Chris insisted when she found Jake clearing up.

'But there's so much to do.'

'And a regiment of staff specially hired to do it.' Chris gave her a push in the direction of her bedroom. 'After what you've been through to-night, you must be exhausted.'

Jake pressed a hand against her back and grimaced. 'I feel as if I've ridden for miles and miles over rough country. Every muscle aches.'

'So what are you waiting for?'

Seeing that Chris wouldn't be deterred, Jake headed for her bedroom. Exhaustion didn't begin to describe her feeling of bone weariness. A shower and bed would be heaven right now.

But there was no refuge in sleep. Over and over, her mind replayed the moment when Nash went down under the slashing blade.

In her dream, it was daylight and there was no flash to blind the attacker. With a banshee shriek, he leapt from the bushes and plunged his knife into Nash's defenceless back. The ground ran red with blood but she was held fast by the fence and no amount of struggling could free her.

'Hang on, Nash, hang on,' she pleaded, willing her sluggish limbs to move. It was like trying to wade through molasses. Gradually she realised that Nash was no longer moving. 'Oh, no!' Her voice rose on a wail of mourning.

Her own cries roused her and she focused on her surroundings with difficulty. Nash hadn't died at all, except in her overwrought imagination. But the vision of him bleeding to death in the chital paddock was so vivid that she knew she wouldn't rest until she saw for herself that he was all right.

As she reached for her dressing-gown, pain lanced through her. Standing in the shower, she'd noticed a mass of bruises from her struggle with the fencing. Her fears for Nash had made her overlook them at the time, but now they felt stiff and sore. She groaned and pressed a splayed hand to her side. It was tempting to sink back into bed but first she needed to satisfy herself that Nash was safe.

The house was dark and quiet, the only sound the dull tock of the grandfather clock in the hall. She had slept for longer than she had first thought. A glance at the clock showed that it was two in the morning.

Nash's room was opposite hers and the door was closed. She padded to it and eased it open. A creaking sound made her catch her breath but there was no sound from inside. Gradually her ears became attuned to the sounds of his breathing. He was asleep.

Holding her breath, she tiptoed into the room. He lay on his back. One arm was angled over his head and the other was at his side, palm upwards. The covers had slipped to his waist, revealing his broad, hair-strewn chest which rose and fell in rhythmic cadence. He slept in the nude, she realised. He had thrust his damaged leg out of the covers and the bandage gleamed in the moonlight. Blood had seeped through it, leaving a brown shadow to indicate where the wound was.

The sight of it made her shudder, evoking memories of her nightmare. It wasn't real, she told herself firmly. He was all right. She focused on the reassuring rise and fall of his chest.

Carefully, she eased his injured leg back on to the bed and slid the covers over it. At the slight movement, he groaned as if it troubled him even in sleep. She watched him anxiously. Was he really sleeping or had he slipped into unconsciousness? Should she call Dr Galen?

His eyes snapped open. 'Jake, what are you doing here?'

'Making sure you're all right,' she said, feeling like a child caught with her hand in the cookie jar. 'I didn't mean to wake you.'

He levered himself up on one elbow. 'What made you feel you had to check on me?'

Her gaze slid away from him and she was glad that he couldn't see the colour staining her cheeks. 'You'll think it's crazy, but I had a bad dream. It seemed so real.'

'I don't think anything of the kind.' He patted the edge of the bed. 'Sit here and tell me about it.'

Tension throbbed through her but she did as he asked. The narrow bed tipped her towards him and she had to grip the edge of the mattress to remain upright. 'It was only a dream,' she insisted.

'About the attack?'

'Yes, only this time I was hung up on the fence and there was nothing I could do. The man with the knife, he…he…' She couldn't go on. Her chest began to heave and her breath came in gulping sobs as the dream images returned with terrifying clarity. 'Oh, Nash, I dreamed that you were dead.'

'Sssh, it's all right. It was only a dream.' He pulled her into his arms and his hand cradled the back of her head as she rested against his chest, trying to still the sobs which wracked her. The bed shook with the force of her shudders and he smoothed a hand across her damp forehead. 'It's the shock, catching up with you. I should have insisted you see the doctor.'

'I feel so silly,' she gasped through her tears. 'I c-can't seem to stop c-crying.'

'Don't try. Let it come out. You'll feel better afterwards.'

As if his approval was all she needed, her tears burst out in a flood, soaking his chest as she clung to him. When it was over, she felt weak but cleansed. She lifted brimming eyes to his face. 'I've never cried like that in my entire life.'

'Maybe you needed to. Not only for what happened tonight, but for your parents. Did you cry for them when they died?'

'Inside. Not outside.'

'Then there was the death of the person you believed yourself to be,' he went on. 'I don't suppose you cried for her, either?'

'I guess not.' She scrubbed at her eyes with the back of her hand. 'I hadn't thought of it as a death, but it was, wasn't it?'

'It was a loss and needs to be properly mourned if you're to come to terms with it.'

She gave him a watery smile. 'I wish it didn't have to hurt so much.'

His hand moved slowly up and down her back, the touch comforting. 'Give it time. I know it hurts now, but it will pass.'

Linking her arms around his neck, she kissed him, putting all of her appreciation for his kindness into the kiss.

It started as a gesture of thanks, but the moment her lips met his a current of electric feeling leapt inside her and she went on kissing him, unable to tear herself away.

His hands slid to her shoulders, his fingers digging into the soft flesh as he pulled her to him. His mouth hardened against hers and tremors shot through her as his tongue flickered against her parted lips. Held against his hard body, she could feel his passion rising, the intensity of her own response catching her by surprise.

His impatient touch stripped the dressing-gown off her shoulders and it fell in a crumpled heap at her waist. Moments later, her nightgown followed and she sat like Venus rising, amid a foaming sea of lacy fabric, her breasts revealed as rosy crescents crowned by starlight.

He gazed at her in wonder. 'Dear heaven, Jake. Have you any idea what you're doing to me?' His rasping voice was stilled as he bent his head to each of her breasts in turn, his tongue tantalising her nipples until their hardness signalled her response. She strained towards him and buried her face against his chest, feeling her body catch fire as his hands wandered down her sides.

Gently, he lifted her on to his lap, pushing the covers aside with a growl of impatience. She sat astride him, every nerve-ending quivering into vibrant life as he caressed her. She had never felt so alive, so possessed, as she did at that moment, and a moan of pleasure ripped from her throat.

His mouth moved over the sensitive skin of her throat and she thrust her head back, revelling in the myriad sensations coursing through her. Fire, ice, pleasure, pain, as well as countless sensations she couldn't even begin to name, followed one another in wave after wave, until she wondered how much more she could endure.

Threading her fingers through his hair, she let them slide down the hard column of his neck, feeling the corded muscles under her hands. How could anyone be so strong yet so gentle? It was just one of the many miracles she treasured about him.

With a groan, he pulled her against his chest. His heartbeat thundered in her ears, playing a wild concerto with her own pulsating heart. Her stomach muscles contracted with longing for him and she felt the small movement. His glittering gaze sought her face. 'Jake?'

'Yes, Nash. Please, yes.'

'I don't want to hurt you in any way.'

'You won't,' she said confidently. He eased her down beside him and she heard him rummaging in a side drawer. His arm was like a steel band around her, while he worked swiftly with the other.

'There's no need for you to do all the worrying,' he said warmly.

His thoughtfulness touched her deeply. In the midst of his passion, he was worried about protecting her. Was there no end to his appeal? She reached for him and her breathing quickened as her fingers grazed the sheathed column of his erection. 'Oh, Nash.'

Rolling on to his side, he caressed her with fierce abandon until she trembled from head to toe like a musical instrument he could play at will, now fast and furious, now gentle and teasing. He seemed to know every nuance of her, as a virtuoso would know a fine violin. The need to have him at the centre of her being, surrounded by all the love she possessed, became both agony and ecstasy.

'Yes, dear heart, yes,' he answered her unspoken plea. His knee slid between her legs and she gripped him with fierce urgency, her senses whirling as the ache to be possessed by him exploded inside her.

'Are you all right, Nash? I heard . . . oh, sorry.' Golden light spilled across their entwined bodies for a brief moment before the door was swiftly closed again. 'I heard a noise. Sorry for the interruption,' came Chris's muffled voice from behind the closed door.

Instantly, Jake sensed a change in Nash. His passion seemed to vanish with the departing footsteps and he swung his legs over the side of the bed and sat up, his back a stony barrier between them.

'Nash, what's the matter?' she probed, not sure what had just happened, only that it had destroyed the harmony between them. 'Chris won't mind. In fact, I think she'd be rather pleased. She's been matchmaking between us ever since we met.'

'Chris may not mind, but I do,' he said tiredly. He sounded like a man emerging from a trance. 'I didn't intend for this to happen.'

'You make it sound wrong,' she protested. He sounded as if he regretted what had passed between them.

'It is, for a lot of reasons.' He began to tick them off on his fingers, his back still turned to her. 'One, you're a guest here, entrusted to my care. And two——'

'Yes, let's hear two,' she demanded before he could continue. Robbed of his fulfilment, she felt cheap and used, growing angry because she couldn't understand why he was doing this. 'On second thoughts, I'll supply two. You're worried that I might actually want something from you. Sex is fine, provided it doesn't lead to commitment because that's the one word that isn't in your vocabulary. Right?'

His furious gaze speared her. 'You seem to have all the answers. Why don't you tell me?'

Pride drove her to continue. 'Well you needn't worry. I don't want anything from a man who feels the way you do.' Her bitter laughter rang between them. 'And I thought you wanted to protect me before we made love. It was really to protect yourself, wasn't it? If I got pregnant, I might have a claim on you and that would never do, would it?'

He shook her fiercely. 'Stop it, Jake. Can't you see, this has happened for the best?'

The best for him, perhaps. For her, it was a painful reminder of how close she had come to giving herself to someone who didn't really want her. 'It's all right, I understand perfectly,' she said stiffly.

Retrieving her nightgown and dressing-gown from the foot of the bed, she dressed slowly, with all the dignity she could muster. 'Goodnight, Nash,' she said. She didn't look at him again as she let herself out.

Chris was buttering a pile of toast when Jake came into the kitchen next morning. Her flushed gaze met Jake's. 'I owe you an apology for last night.'

'It wasn't your fault. You thought you heard a noise.'

'I was worried about Nash. If I'd known he was in such good hands, I wouldn't have bothered.'

Jake reached for the percolator and poured coffee into a cup, her shakiness causing her to spill some on to the counter. 'Oh, damn,' she muttered, reaching for a cloth to mop it up.

Chris regarded her in concern. 'Is something the matter, I mean besides my *faux pas* last night?'

'I'm all right, really,' Jake insisted. 'If you must know, last night was a mistake. You saved me from making it much worse.'

'This sounds like Nash talking, not you at all.'

'It *is* Nash talking, and he's probably right. I'd be a fool to get involved with someone who hates commitment as much as he does.'

Chris passed her some toast. 'And *are* you a fool, Jake?'

'If you mean, have I already fallen for him, yes, I'm that big a fool.'

'Oh, Jake. I'm so sorry. If any of this is my fault...'

'It isn't,' Jake assured her. 'I managed it all by myself. But thanks to you, the damage isn't as bad as it could have been. I can leave Wirrinda with some shred of my self-respect intact.'

'I ought to kill that brother of mine,' Chris said fiercely. 'He knows so much about nature and not a thing about human nature. He doesn't care who he hurts.'

Jake tossed her head in denial. Nash might not care where she was concerned, but for Chris herself, he cared more than she knew. Protecting his sister was a much higher priority than guarding Jake's feelings. All the same, she couldn't let Chris believe the worst of him. 'He cares,' she said flatly. 'Believe me, he cares, only not about me.'

Chris's speculative look followed her out of the kitchen.

CHAPTER SEVEN

'YOU can tell Col Galen what he can do with his rest. I'm getting up and that's that.'

Jake almost collided with Chris as she rocketed out of Nash's room. Her face was flushed and her hands shook as she clutched an untouched breakfast tray.

'Problems with your patient?' Jake surmised, glancing towards the closed door.

Chris rolled her eyes heavenwards. 'I'd rather bring a jumbo jet in to land on one engine than cope with him in this mood.'

'Would you like me to try?'

'You're doing far too much already,' Chris said reprovingly. 'It was after eleven when I went to bed and the office light was still burning.'

'With Nash out of action, there's a lot to do.'

'But surely you don't have to do it all? You're out riding all day then spending whole evenings hunched over the computer. It can't be doing you any good.'

'I'm surviving,' Jake demurred. 'Besides, the extra workload is my own idea. I don't want Nash coming back to find a backlog.'

Chris clucked her tongue. 'I hope he appreciates your devotion to duty.'

It was unlikely, as Nash had no idea how hard she'd been working since he was injured a week ago. Fortunately Chris had been able to take some holidays to help with the running of the house. This freed Jake to cope with the outdoor work and handling the routine office work.

Mastering the station's computer system had been a challenge. By spending her nights with her head buried in manuals the size of telephone books, she had finally managed to unravel the system's mysteries. As a result, the all-important deer-breeding databank was up to date, as well as most of the day-to-day paperwork.

She massaged her eyes which stung after another late night spent staring at the computer screen. The five hours' sleep she'd managed felt like five minutes. 'Did I hear Nash say he was getting up?' she asked.

Chris gave a long-suffering sigh. 'Everyone for miles must have heard him. I've tried to get him to follow Dr Galen's orders, but short of tying him to the bed I can't do much more.'

'Then maybe it's time he was up and about.' For herself, Jake wouldn't be sorry to have him back in action. She wasn't sure how much longer she could keep up the gruelling pace she'd set for herself. 'How is his leg?'

'Well enough to kick a chair across the room,' Chris said dourly.

'He must be improving. Why don't you call the doctor? If he gives Nash the green light, you're off the hook.'

Chris flashed her a grateful smile. 'You're a genius. Are you sure you won't marry my brother and settle here permanently?'

'What, and suffer the way you've done the last few days?' Jake kept her tone jocular but couldn't quite suppress the pang which shot through her as she spoke.

'You're right. I couldn't do it to a friend.'

Their eyes met and Jake was conscious of the warmth in the other woman's gaze. In the short time they had known each other, a bond had been forged. Perhaps it had always been there, waiting to be recognised. It was all the more remarkable because Chris had no idea of its source.

'I'd better get back to work,' Jake said, breaking the spell.

'Don't overdo it, will you?'

Jake stifled a yawn. 'I'll try not to.'

But it was difficult to keep her promise when there was so much work to be done. As well as keeping track of the breeding programme, the computer was used for budgeting, feedlotting, share trading and stock management.

Coupling the computer to the telephone system put Nash in touch with the rest of the world. In seconds, he could call up anything from Chicago live cattle prices to the number of sheep on feedlot in the USA at any time.

Virtually every station activity was recorded in a daily diary rather like a ship's log, while future tasks were shown on a yearly planning log.

Once a month, farm expenses and income had to be recorded and compared to previous seasons to show the ongoing state of Wirrinda's finances.

It was an impressive system and Jake was glad she'd taken a computer course at Texas A & M. If only she hadn't been so tired from keeping up with her other duties, she would have loved working with the system.

She was entering the current week's expenses when the green lettering on the screen began to swim before her eyes. Flicking the screen off, she sat back in Nash's chair and massaged her eyes. In contrast to the computer, the chair was an antique, a tilting model with worn wooden arms polished to a soft patina, and studded leather upholstery. It must have belonged to several generation of Campbells, she thought, running an appreciative hand over the silky timber. How often had Nash sat where she was sitting now?

In her drowsy, half-awake state, she imagined that he came into the office and stood looking down at her. Through half-closed lids, she saw him as if he was actually beside her. The corners of her mouth tugged upwards into a dreamy smile of contentment.

'What the blazes do you think you're doing?'

Reality came crashing in on her and her eyelids snapped open. 'Nash? What are you doing here? You should be in bed,' she said stupidly.

'You prefer me out of the way, don't you?' he demanded. 'So you could make free with my files for your own benefit.'

Her drowsiness vanished as she leapt to her feet. 'I was doing no such thing.'

'Then how do you explain these?'

His sweeping gesture encompassed a pile of folders which littered the desktop. They were marked 'Campbell family—private' and tabbed with the names of each family member. They had been in her way when she was searching for some information on lot feeding and she had simply piled them on the desk to be returned to the filing cabinet later.

'I didn't read them. They were in my way,' she explained, seeing how it looked to him.

'We're all in your way, aren't we, Jake? You came here for one reason and one reason only. My accident must have suited your purpose admirably.'

Hot colour raged up her cheeks and she pressed the backs of her hands to her face to cool it. 'You're crazy! If I'd wanted you out of the way, I wouldn't have intervened when the rustler tried to stab you.'

There was a pause during which he mastered his anger with an obvious effort. 'You did save my life and I should thank you for it.'

'There's no need. I did what anyone would have done.'

'All the same, I *am* grateful. But it doesn't mean you can take advantage of my absence to go on with your private research. Or delegate your work to Chris just because she happens to have some free time.'

'What?'

'You heard me. I notice that Chris has been taking care of the house while you've been on your wild-goose chase through the family files.'

The accusation was so unjust that she began to laugh. Once she started, she was unable to stop. Soon her whole body shook as the harsh sounds bubbled up from her throat and tears coursed down her cheeks. Exhaustion seemed to have robbed her of all self-control.

'Stop it, Jake!' Nash's command carried the force of a whip-crack but it had no effect. The mad laughter continued to wrack her slender body.

Through her tears she saw him limp around the desk and raise his hand. Once, twice his palm cracked across her cheek, the blows flinging her head first to one side then the other.

The blows had their desired effect. She reeled back, clutching a hand to her stinging cheek, as the laughter finally died in her throat, replaced by distressed sobs.

He was at her side in an instant but this time, he gathered her into his arms and smoothed the hair away from her eyes. 'Sssh, it's all right. I didn't want to do that but you were hysterical.'

She struggled free of his grasp and fumbled for a handkerchief to blot her streaming eyes. 'I'm sorry for breaking down,' she responded. 'It's becoming a bad habit around you.'

'I'd rather dry your tears than cope with hysteria,' he said shortly. His hand came up again but as she flinched away he gave a throaty sound of impatience and touched the back of his hand to her cheek. 'You should bathe your face in cold water. I'd never forgive myself if I bruised you.'

'Some people don't know their own strength,' she said with an attempt at lightness.

He frowned. 'Don't joke about it, Jake. I'm not in the habit of striking women.' His hands pressed down on her shoulders, forcing her into his chair. 'Now tell me what this is all about.'

'I wasn't snooping through your files. I only moved them aside to get something else I needed.'

He perched on the edge of the desk, massaging his injured leg. 'But what are you doing in here at all?'

'Keeping up with the paperwork.'

'As well as your outdoor tasks?'

'Yes.'

He gave a low whistle and reached across to the computer keyboard in front of her. Deftly, he pressed several keys and the screen sprang to life. Numbers scrolled up it and he regarded them in astonishment. When he snapped the computer off, his face was grim. 'It seems as if I've misjudged you.'

'I tried to tell you.'

'Yes, you did, but I saw only the worst possibility. It never even occurred to you to look up your own history, did it?'

'No.' She had been much too busy to think of her own needs. Six weeks had passed and she was no nearer to solving the mystery of her roots than she had been when she arrived.

'Now I know what an honest-to-goodness louse feels like,' he said harshly.

'Don't, please. It was a misunderstanding.'

'But it drove you to the brink of hysteria.' His breath hissed out in a sigh of disgust. 'You must be exhausted, if you've been doing all this as well as your own job.'

She inclined her head. 'I didn't realise how much there was to running a place this size.'

'So Chris looked after the house while you ran Wirrinda?'

Her hands lifted expressively. 'I couldn't have done it without Chris. Len and the men were at the muster camp and we couldn't let everything pile up here.'

'You mean *you* couldn't let it pile up,' contradicted a voice from the doorway. Chris came into the room and confronted Nash, her arms folded aggressively across her chest. 'I can't take any credit. It was Jake's doing and I trust you'll show her your appreciation.'

There was a tense pause as Jake thought of how Nash had shown his appreciation. Her head was still ringing and she was sure her cheeks carried the marks of his fingers. She ducked her head before Chris could see them.

'I would like to show Jake my appreciation,' Nash said to Chris, but his lowered voice was directed at Jake. 'There's a cattle sale in Seymour at the end of the week. Perhaps Jake would like to see it.'

'Some holiday!' Chris snorted in amusement. 'Can't you see she's wrecked? I'll bet she hasn't had a day off since she got here.'

'I would like to see the cattle sale,' Jake intervened before Chris could say any more. 'It will give me a break and a chance to see how you run a cattle sale here.'

'Then it's settled,' Nash agreed. 'I'll take you myself.'

In shocked surprise, Jake stared at him. '*You're* taking me? But what about your leg?'

'When the doctor checked me over, he suggested I use my leg as much as I can to prevent the muscles stiffening up. I'll have him put it in writing if you like.'

'I believe you.' Misgivings coloured her voice. When he'd suggested that she should attend the cattle sale, she had seen a golden chance to visit the town archives and try to learn more about her family. Finding that Nash meant to accompany her himself filled her with a mixture of pleasure and apprehension.

'Since you insist on a busman's holiday, I hope you'll take Jake out for a slap-up dinner in Seymour. It's the least you can do after all the work she's done around here.'

Nerves fluttered in Jake's stomach. This idea was rapidly getting out of hand. 'I don't need any more thanks for doing my job.'

'Nevertheless, it's a good idea,' Nash concurred. He probably saw it as a way to make amends for misjudging her. 'So pack your glad rags.'

Her baffled gaze met his. 'Excuse me?'

'Your finery, prom dress, whatever they call it in Texas,' Chris explained. 'Seymour may be small but it has some good restaurants. And hotels,' she added significantly.

Jake's heart began to race in earnest. Couldn't Chris see that her attempts at matchmaking would only make Nash more determined not to get involved?

'We won't be staying overnight, will we?' she asked him, afraid that she already knew the answer.

'I don't see why not. As Chris says, you've earned a break.' He favoured Chris with a broad grin. 'Does that satisfy your requirements?'

His sister looked smug. 'Better. Much better.'

At Nash's insistence, Jake took the next few days off. Len and the others were back from the muster camp and Nash was running the office, so there was less for her to do, and she used the time to ride around the station, filling her notebook with ideas and observations which John could use in Texas.

She also caught up on her letters home. John had already written several times expressing his concern for her. She tried to reassure him but she was sure he saw through her. He knew how much this quest meant to her. He also feared that if she found what she was looking for she wouldn't come back to Corpus Christi. Since she didn't know the answer herself yet, there was no way she could set his mind at rest.

'You didn't have to do this,' she told Nash when they were finally on the way to Seymour in his Range Rover. 'I'm sure Len or one of the men would have gladly taken me to the cattle sale.'

'Has it occurred to you that I might *want* to?' he asked, his gaze flickering from the road to her and back again. 'It was the least I could do under the circumstances.'

Although she suspected that the trip was a peace offering rather than because he wanted to spend time alone with her, she felt disappointed. She shifted restlessly, tugging at the seat belt which angled across her breasts. 'I could go back to the Caseys now,' she dropped into the silence. 'Bill is much better. I could be of help to them.'

Her peripheral vision caught the tightening of his hands on the steering-wheel. 'Do you want to leave, Jake?'

'What I want isn't the issue.'

His exasperated sigh hissed between them as he drew another wrong conclusion. 'Can't you forget that adoption business for one minute? What if you never find your real family?'

'Then I'll have to live with it, won't I?' Anger at his lack of understanding charged her tone. He

had no idea that he was the real source of her dis-
contentment. With Nash in her future, she could
have lived with anything the past revealed. Or
nothing, if that was how it turned out. Without
him, both her past and her future were equally
empty. One or the other had to be filled somehow.

'People who dig into the past tend to find skeletons,' he continued.

Her startled gaze flew to his face. 'You sound as
if you expect me to find some.'

'In a situation like this, it's almost inevitable.'

A sudden suspicion made her angle her body
towards him. 'Do you know more than you've told
me?'

'I know that you and Chris were born around
here and split up at birth to be raised by two different mothers,' he said evenly. 'Anything else is
pure speculation on my part.'

He *did* know something which he was keeping
from her. Or else he had guessed part of the story.
'You wouldn't care to share your speculations with
me?' she asked.

'No, I wouldn't.'

He forestalled further questions by switching the
conversation to the cattle sale at Seymour. Sim-
mering with annoyance, she barely listened as he
described how an Australian cattle sale worked. But
in spite of herself, she became interested. 'In Texas,
we have an arena where the buyers sit to inspect
the cattle as they're led past. Don't you have anything like that?'

'No such luxury. As you'll see shortly, the yards
are divided into fenced pens with walkways all
around the top of them. You walk along these to

inspect the lots. This one is a store sale, for breeding stock. We also have fat sales, for beef cattle.'

'Are you buying?' she queried, tucking the new terms into her mental file.

He shook his head. 'This is strictly for your education. In any case, I've decided to get out of the cattle business to concentrate on deer farming and grain production. It makes sense when you consider that the grain used to produce one hamburger can feed a human being for two days.'

'Makes you wonder how much longer we can go on feeding the world's grain to livestock,' she observed, 'when it takes seven pounds of grain to produce one of beef.'

There was respect in his glance when he looked at her. 'Are you interested in futures studies?'

'How can a rancher *not* be interested when world food supplies are at stake?'

'You'd be surprised,' he said drily. 'Not everyone takes such a far-sighted attitude.'

He sounded both pleased and surprised that she shared his concern. For herself, she didn't find it unusual. They shared so many interests already. If only he felt the same way about commitment as she did, it would be so easy. But one of the things she'd learned as a futurist was to accept what was, rather than wish for the moon. And right now Nash Campbell had a lot in common with the moon.

Her gloomy thoughts were dispelled when they arrived at Seymour, a thriving commercial centre surrounded by the rich river flats of the Murrumbidgee Valley.

For a century and a half it had been a popular camping spot for teamsters and their heavily laden bullock wagons. In the 1800s, bushrangers were drawn to the town by the lure of the gold mined in the surrounding districts. According to her studies, many a miner had been relieved of his find by people like Ben Hall and Captain Moonlight.

Now Seymour was a friendly, bustling town which reminded Jake of her home town. Like Corpus Christi, which followed the curve of a bay, Seymour followed a winding river so few of its streets ran straight. Corpus, too, got its start as a tent city, housing the US army in the long-ago war against Mexico.

The only thing Seymour lacked was the endless stretch of white sand known as North Beach, where Jake had learned to surf some of the most challenging waves in Texas.

Two fingers snapped in front of her eyes. 'Planning to sit in the car all day?'

Blinking rapidly, she shook her head. 'I was comparing your town with where I come from.'

'You're forgetting something,' he said with an odd catch in his voice. 'This *is* where you come from.'

Oh, lord, she *had* forgotten. This was where she was born. Her eyes began to mist and she made a show of collecting her things so he wouldn't see how strongly the reminder had affected her.

There was no need to ask where the sale was being held. The dust and clamour was all around them. She followed Nash as he made his way towards a forest of timber pens.

There was a squeal of excitement then someone hurtled into Jake's line of vision. 'Hi, you-all. You made it after all.'

Jake fought back a leaden sensation which filled her at the sight of her fellow countrywoman. 'Susan, how're you doing?'

Susan linked her arm companionably through Nash's. 'I'm fine. Nash here was kind enough to tell me about the sale at your birthday party. I told him I'd do my darnedest to be here.'

With sickening certainty, Jake saw why Nash had been so keen to come. He wasn't accommodating her at all. He was keeping a date with Susan. Jake wished he had told her outright instead of pretending it was on her account.

Susan smiled up at Nash and the sight twisted something inside Jake. 'How's the leg?' she heard Susan ask.

'Healing,' he told her. 'Jake's been doing my share of the work while I recovered.'

Susan favoured her with a tiny smile. 'How sweet. You must be stir-crazy after being shut up inside all week, Nash. I'll have to make it up to you.'

She was so obvious that Jake felt sick. In a strange way, she almost felt sorry for Susan, knowing that the harder she chased Nash, the more elusive he would become.

Oddly enough, he didn't seem to mind Susan's attention. 'If you're on your own, why don't you join us while we look over the stock,' he suggested.

Susan positively glowed. 'That's a perfectly fine idea.'

The walkways above the sale yards were narrow, giving Jake little choice but to follow the other two. Susan kept her arm through Nash's and hung on his every word as he explained what was going on. Now and again he turned to include Jake in the explanation but she had the feeling that if she wandered off, she would hardly be missed.

When the sale was over, she put her theory to the test, suggesting that she would visit the town archives and find her own way to their hotel afterwards.

'Don't you worry about Nash, I'll take good care of him,' Susan said, her eyes bright with enthusiasm.

But Nash frowned. 'I planned to show you around this afternoon, but if the research is more important to you——'

'It is,' she said firmly. She had no intention of trailing around after the two of them all day. 'I have my bearings now so I won't get lost.'

'Very well. I'll see you at the hotel at six, then.'

Why did he sound so angry, Jake wondered, watching them walk away? Was it because she had taken the initiative? He was probably better off with Susan. At least she had her priorities clearly established. Not for her the torment of wondering who she was and where she came from.

Susan might even break through Nash's reserve, where Jake had failed. The thought made her want to run after them and tear Susan's hand off his arm in a frenzy of possessiveness. But common sense stayed her feet. When they were at college together, Susan's motto had been 'plenty more where he came from'. Even if her pursuit of Nash proved fruitless, she wouldn't nurse a broken heart for long. And Nash himself might appreciate Susan's free and easy attitude towards romance since it **dovetailed so** neatly with his own aversion to **commitment.**

It made perfect sense, so why wasn't Jake pleased about it, instead of feeling utterly desolate?

The best solution seemed to be to immerse herself in work. However, her search of the town's register of births, deaths and marriages turned up no more information than she already possessed. Except for one puzzling anomaly.

She approached the clerk with her problem. 'Your records show that Jacqueline Christine McVey was born here on this date.' She showed him the microfiche entry. 'But her sister isn't mentioned at all.'

'No problem,' he said with a grin. He had already tried to arrange a date with her and her refusal hadn't fazed him in the slightest. 'It means she doesn't have one.'

'But I know she does,' Jake persisted. 'By coincidence, her name is also Christine.'

The clerk frowned. 'Records can be wrong, but mainly in the early days when spelling was hit or miss. These days, it's unlikely that one sister could be registered and not the other. Are these people relatives of yours?'

'The Australian branch of the family,' she supplied hastily. His interest in her was becoming unnerving and she needed to escape before he asked questions she couldn't answer. 'I guess I must have my facts wrong,' she said with a sigh of resignation.

He pushed a pad of paper towards her and leaned closer. 'Look, I'm not supposed to do this but I'll see what I can dig up for you if you write all the details down there. Tracing living family members can be harder than tracing dead ones.'

She made a show of consulting her watch. 'I appreciate your help but I have to rush. I'll let you know when I'll be in town again.'

His admiring glance swept over her. 'I'd like that. Where did you say you were staying?'

Over her shoulder, she smiled but ignored his question. She had carefully avoided any mention of where she was living. 'I must rush. Thanks for everything.'

She could feel his bewilderment following her out of the door. Outside, she propped herself against a wall and let out a sigh of relief. She hadn't learned much but she hadn't given herself away, either. The clerk had no idea why she was interested in those particular records. She hadn't broken her promise to Nash.

At the same time, questions buzzed in her brain. Why was she the only one of the twins whose birth was registered? While the clerk was answering a telephone call, she had sneaked a look at the listings for Campbell and there was no Christine Campbell listed there, either.

Nash could be mistaken about their relationship. Maybe they weren't sisters at all, far less twins. But it didn't explain the absence of any records for Chris. Nor could Jake deny the strength of the bond which existed between her and Chris. They both felt it, although Chris didn't know why. And they were alike in so many ways that they *had* to be related.

The only person who could answer the questions burning in her head was Nash's mother, Alice

Campbell, the one source which was denied to her. Frustration gnawed at her as she made her way back to the hotel.

CHAPTER EIGHT

THE century-old Seymour Hotel was comfortable and unpretentious with heavy oak furniture and high-ceilinged rooms furnished with hand-carved bedsteads, washstands and tapestry-covered chairs. Jake fingered the old-fashioned lace bedspread. It was like being in the Australia of a century ago.

The age of the building meant that the bathrooms were located along the hall. They were delightful, with deep, claw-footed tubs and brass fittings. Jake lay in the tub for a long time, letting the scented water soak away her frustrations. The water had started to cool when she remembered her appointment with Nash. She was hurrying down the hall when he intercepted her.

His appreciative glance took in her bare feet and glowing skin. 'So that's where you were. I knocked on your door and got no answer. I thought you were asleep and wondered if I should awaken you with a kiss.'

He was joking but the idea made the blood sing in her veins. It was just as well her skin colour was already heightened from the bath. 'I forgot the time,' she said.

'No problem. We aren't due to meet Susan and Scott for half an hour yet.'

Under the towel turbanning her damp hair, her eyebrows arched. 'Who is Scott?'

'Scott Howard is the son of the owners of Kookaburrah, Susan's hosts,' he explained. 'We ran into him on the way back from the sale and I invited him and Susan to join us for dinner. I hope you don't mind.'

'There goes my intimate dinner for two,' she said, her jocular tone masking her disappointment. She *had* been looking forward to dining with Nash alone.

'You'll like Scott,' he went on. 'He's a former International Agricultural Association trainee. He spent some time in Texas so you two should have a lot to talk about.'

Jake swallowed hard as understanding came. She was supposed to partner Scott, leaving Nash free to entertain Susan. Suddenly the evening had lost its appeal. She made a mental plan to finish dinner quickly then escape to her room. Playing gooseberry wasn't her style, and she was not going to be foisted on to a complete stranger to enable Nash to play the field.

He took the key dangling from her fingers and opened her door for her, then leaned against the door-jamb with his arms folded. 'What are you planning to wear tonight?'

Did it matter, since it was for Scott, not him? 'I haven't decided. How formal is the dining-room here?'

'Reasonably formal and the chef has an excellent reputation. Why not wear that black thing with the lace? The one you wore for International Night at the Ag. College.'

'You remember that?' Her topaz eyes widened with astonishment.

His finger touched the point of her chin. 'I remember everything you've worn. But especially the black.'

Her heart beat wildly for a moment before she brought it under control. He probably said the same thing to lots of girls, safe in the knowledge that he wouldn't be called to account by any of them. Maybe he'd even said it to Susan Rand.

The thought gave her the strength to muster a careless laugh. 'I didn't pack the black dress, sorry.'

His sea-green gaze clouded. 'Pity.' Then he moved away. 'Well, I'm sure whatever you brought will be fine. I'll meet you in the lobby in half an hour.'

Damn, she thought as she closed the door and leaned against it with her eyes shut. She *had* brought the black dress but she wasn't wearing it to make herself more appealing for Scott Howard, if it was what Nash had in mind. Putting cattle on display for potential buyers was one thing, but he couldn't treat her the same way.

In defiance, she pulled on a pair of plain black evening trousers over a severely tailored white blouse whose only decoration was a row of tiny pearl buttons down the front. Twisting her hair into a knot, she fastened it at the nape of her neck and clipped plain pearl earrings to her lobes. There. Nash could parade her before Scott if he wanted to, but she wasn't going to dress herself up to make it easy for him.

Keeping her make-up deliberately light, she used eau-de-Cologne instead of her usual Chanel perfume. Would Nash even notice the difference?

Glancing at herself in the full-length mirror, she was dismayed to see that, far from making her look plain and unattractive, the tailored trousers emphasised her small waist and narrow hips, making her legs seem a mile long. The cut of the blouse made her breasts appear fuller and higher. It wasn't the effect she had intended but there was no time to change. It seemed as if Nash was going to win this round, after all.

'You look stunning,' he said when she met him in the lobby. Susan was already there. She greeted Jake warmly but her eyes hardly left Nash. From behind Susan, a six-foot, blond-haired man stepped forward and held out his hand.

Jake was conscious of being under inspection as Nash performed the introductions. But the other man's pale blue eyes sparkled with friendliness and his grip was firm as he shook her hand. 'Delighted to meet you, Miss McVey.'

'Jake, please. It's short for Jacqueline,' she explained, liking this wide-shouldered Aussie almost against her will. 'Susan speaks highly of Kookaburrah,' she added.

Scott's gaze flickered to the top of Susan's head, which was bent as she listened to Nash. Scott cared for Susan, Jake realised with a jolt. His wistful look was quickly masked, but not before she had seen what it meant. 'Are all the trainees as pretty as you two this year?' he asked.

If she hadn't intercepted his revealing look, Jake would have taken his compliment at face value. But it was really meant for Susan. 'I'm not sure the guys would like to hear you say that,' she said as a tight band of pain wound itself around her heart.

It seemed unfair that Susan had captured the hearts of both men so effortlessly. She was glad when Nash suggested that they go in to dinner.

He had reserved a table in a quiet corner of the restaurant. It was a busy evening, the tables occupied by farmers, here for the cattle sale, and now treating their families to a rare night out. Like their counterparts in Texas, they welcomed a break from the dawn-to-dusk grind of farm life.

As in the rest of the hotel, the restaurant had a warm, old-fashioned feel with lace curtains, an open fireplace, and thick red carpeting. The bar along one side was adorned with items from yester-year, handcuffs, lanterns and old hand-pumps from Seymour's gold-mining past.

A three-piece band played quietly in a far corner and a sigh bubbled in Jake's throat. Such a dreamy, romantic setting demanded a partner who felt the same way.

Not that Scott wasn't attentive and pleasant. He entertained her with anecdotes about life at Kookaburrah, which was predominantly a cattle station. But his gaze kept straying to Susan, and Jake noticed how often he mentioned the other girl's name in his conversation.

According to the menu, the hotel specialised in serving local produce. Jake chose a pea and lettuce soup to start. As a main course, she chose medallions of beef in a green peppercorn sauce, trying not to think too much about the cattle milling around in the pens that morning.

When they reached the dessert stage, Scott handed Susan the menu, but before she could open it he asked, 'Have you tried pavlova yet?'

'The dancer?'

'In Australia, it's a dessert, almost a national dish in fact. They take a meringue base and fill it with freshly whipped cream, strawberries and kiwi fruit.'

Susan groaned. 'It's heavenly, but disaster for the diet.'

'I shouldn't have thought it would worry you,' Scott said, his gaze roving over Susan's lithe figure.

'It's not, provided I keep active,' she said with a meaningful glance at Nash.

Jake wanted to kick her under the table. Couldn't she see how distressed Scott was by the attention she was paying to Nash? Scott was her host, after all. At the same time, Jake accepted that she had her own reasons for wanting Susan to pay more attention to Scott, plain old-fashioned jealousy being the main one.

It was something she and Scott had in common. Sympathy for him prompted her to be nicer to him. He was easy to talk to and laughed readily when she reminded him of his visit to Texas.

'Everything you touch is prickly there,' he recalled. 'I'll never forget my first encounter with the "wait-a-minute bush" in the Trans Pecos.'

'It's named because every hiker who gets caught yells out "wait a minute" while he tries to get free,' she echoed, laughing. 'Remember the pencil cactus?'

He rubbed his behind in a rueful gesture. 'They have those funny little green cylinders which cling to your clothes, only letting you know they're there when you try to sit down.'

'Don't I know it! Did you try Tex-Mex food?'

Scott rolled his eyes. 'When my host described it as hot as the hinges of Hell's front door, I thought he was exaggerating.'

She laughed. 'You'd have been safer with corn dogs or chicken-fried steaks.' A wave of home-sickness abruptly rolled over her and she took a quick sip of wine. 'Texas is a world of its own, isn't it, Susan?'

'I don't miss it at all,' the other girl said pointedly. 'For me, Australia has one great compensation—Australian men.'

When she looked directly at Nash, Scott got to his feet. The band was playing an upbeat dance tune and he held out his hand to Jake. 'Would you like to dance?'

Susan smiled at Nash. 'Now there's a fine idea.'

'I'll have to let my food settle first,' Jake said, afraid that her kindness to Scott might have given him the wrong idea. He looked woebegone as he sat down again.

Susan's smile favoured Nash. 'What about you?'

He rubbed his injured leg significantly. 'Dancing's out for me for the time being. Why don't you and Scott go ahead? Jake and I can keep each other company.'

Scott's face was a study in pleased surprise. 'Shall we?'

Less eagerly but with good grace, Susan accepted his hand and they moved on to the minuscule dance floor. When they spun away, Nash turned to Jake. 'What were you two getting so cosy about?'

He sounded annoyed. She was puzzled. Wasn't she supposed to pair off with Scott? 'We were reminiscing about Texas. He lived there as an agricultural exchange trainee.'

Nash stared morosely into his wine glass. 'You know that he's attracted to Susan?'

'So I noticed, but I didn't think you did.'

'Why do you think I invited him along tonight?'

Her brain reeled. Scott had been invited for Susan's sake? A flood of remorse washed over her and she felt ashamed of trying to make herself look unattractive. She had been certain that Nash had invited Scott to divert Jake while Nash busied himself with Susan, but it seemed she was totally wrong. Of course, it didn't mean that Susan agreed with his strategy. As far as Jake could see, Susan only had eyes for Nash. What a tangled web it was.

'That was a deep sigh,' Nash said, hearing her soft out-pouring of breath. 'Didn't your research go well today?'

She pressed her palms over her eyes and shook her head. 'I don't know what I expected but it wasn't the dead end I found. Without a court order, I can't get access to my original birth certificate and the one on record only shows the names of my adoptive parents.'

'Isn't the fact that your adoptive parents are gone taken into account?'

'Only if I can prove that my natural parents are also deceased.' Her mouth drooped at the corners. 'And I can't prove it. I don't know who they are.'

'So there's nothing more you can do?'

Her fingers curled into a fist on the table. 'There must be a way, and I'm going to keep looking until I find it.'

He stirred cream into his coffee and concentrated on the milky spiral. 'What's the point? You're only making yourself miserable.'

She leaned forward so abruptly that her coffee spilled into the saucer. She ignored it and fastened her angry gaze on him. 'I suppose you'd prefer me to give up, wouldn't you? Then I wouldn't disturb your world. But it's already disturbed and if I don't solve the mystery, some day, someone else will.'

His hard gaze bored into her. 'You'd better say what you mean.'

Tears filmed her topaz eyes and her voice shook with emotion but she refused to give in to it. 'Today I stumbled on a flaw in your perfect family. Thanks to a clerk at the court-house, who told me more than he should have done, I discovered that there's no record of Chris's birth at all.'

A frown etched a V into his forehead. 'There must be. She has a pilot's licence and a passport. Maybe the clerk meant you couldn't see her records because she's adopted.'

Her head swung violently from side to side. 'It was the first thing I thought of but there are no records for Chris, adopted or otherwise.'

'Hell's bells.' A low whistle punctuated his words. 'It must be a clerical error. I *know* my mother has Chris's birth certificate.'

'Have you ever seen it?'

'No,' he admitted slowly. 'She gave Chris a copy which she uses when she needs it.'

'But if it isn't on record...'

'Then it probably isn't genuine.' He gave another low whistle. 'What a mess.'

Leaning forward, she reached for his hand. 'Nash, if I could only talk to your mother. She's the only one who can give us any answers.'

His fingers almost crushed hers in an iron grip. 'You may want answers, I don't. Why can't you leave well alone?'

The tears crowding her eyes threatened to spill over but she contained them. 'Can't you see what this means to me? It's all very well for you. You probably come from a long line of Campbells who've lived at Wirrinda forever. Can you imagine what it's like to have a great, gaping hole in your past?'

'You're wrong about the Campbells,' he said tautly. 'I was about six when we moved here. My father owned a market garden near Milperra in Sydney. When the area was re-zoned for housing, he made enough money to buy Wirrinda with a hefty mortgage. I stayed with my grandmother in Sydney while they settled in. Chris arrived while I was away.

'Country towns being what they are, it was years before we were accepted as locals. So it's hardly the multi-generational saga you're imagining.'

It also explained how his mother was able to adopt Chris without causing comment in the district. From what she knew of farming communities, gossip travelled like wildfire, so it seemed inconceivable that the arrival of a new child could go unnoticed.

'All the same, you know where you came from. When your children ask about their roots, you'll tell them what you told me. What am I supposed to tell mine?'

Before Nash could frame an answer, she jumped to her feet and snatched up her bag. 'Excuse me. I'm not feeling very well suddenly. I'm going to turn in.'

'Jake, wait.'

But she couldn't endure any more of his reasoned arguments about why she was wasting her time. She didn't blame him for wanting to protect his family but he might try to see her side. If she stayed he would see how hurt she was by his stubbornness and it might give away the depth of her feelings for him.

Pride was all she had left. It wasn't much of a shield against a man who only took without giving, which was the unvarnished way of looking at his aversion to commitment. She made herself face it as she plodded back up the stairs to her room. For the first time, she made herself see his attitude in its true light, as an excuse for avoiding any woman who tried to bind him with her love.

It was her own fault. Jean had tried to warn her about Nash. But she had never intended to fall in love with him. It had happened while she was distracted by her search. Now she had to make it unhappen and she hadn't a clue how to go about it.

Flinging aside her evening clothes which hadn't achieved their goal after all, she shrugged on a boldly patterned housecoat she had bought in Hawaii. The bright floral design mocked her bleak mood but she had nothing else with her so it would have to do. She sat down at the dressing table and reached for the cold cream to remove her make-up.

A knock at the door stilled her hand. 'Who is it?'

'I came to make sure you were all right.'

Nash had followed her upstairs. 'I'm fine, thanks. You can go back to the others with a clear conscience.'

'Not until I see for myself that you aren't ill.'

Opening the door a crack, she peered out. The sight of Nash standing in the hallway, his broad-shouldered frame dominating the narrow space, almost shattered her resolve. She made herself say calmly, 'As you can see, I'm fine. Thanks for checking on me.'

She began to close the door but his foot slid into the opening. 'Damn it, I care about you, Jake. You're practically part of my own family.'

The ache inside her was almost more than she could bear. She didn't want to be another sister to him, to be put into a slot where she wouldn't make demands beyond those of a family member. It might suit him, but she was the one who would pay the price.

There was only one solution and that was to go back where she came from and try to pick up the pieces of her life, the pieces to which she had access, anyway. She hugged her robe around herself. 'I was about to go to bed.'

'Then you *are* ill?'

'No, honestly. I had a trying time at the court-house and it all got on top of me. I'll be fine after a night's rest.'

His focus narrowed and the intensity of his gaze made the hairs lift on the back of her neck. 'If you change your mind and want to talk, I'll be right next door.'

She had expected him to rejoin the others. 'Isn't Susan expecting you back?' she asked him in surprise.

An impatient sigh punctuated his reply. 'Why should she? When the dancing's over, Scott will see her back to her hotel.'

'Scott will like that,' she said, although it wouldn't necessarily please Susan. But she shouldn't be surprised. Nash was good at arranging people's lives with the least amount of inconvenience to himself. He must have noticed Susan's interest in him and had neatly deflected it in Scott's direction. The man had a genius for avoiding entanglements. 'Is there anything else?' she asked tiredly.

He seemed reluctant to leave, as if there was more that he wanted to say but couldn't or wouldn't. 'Goodnight, Jake,' he said at last. 'Sleep well.'

Faint hope, she thought as she closed the door again. Sleep was the last thing she felt like, although she was tired after the cattle sale and her visit to the court-house. Maybe a shower would relax her enough for sleep.

The hallway was dim and quiet as she padded along it carrying her sponge-bag and towel. Passing Nash's door, she paused and listened but no sound came from the other side. Had he gone back to the restaurant after all? The idea depressed her and she quickened her steps.

In the bathroom she slipped off her housecoat, splashed cool water on to her face and scrubbed her teeth until they gleamed. Tugging the shower curtain across the bath, she saw it—the biggest, hairiest spider she had ever encountered.

The size of a saucer, it was like something out of a nightmare as it crouched in the bottom of the bath. In another second, her bare foot would have touched it.

The scream which tore from her throat was driven by mindless reaction. The sound bounced off the tiled walls, echoing and re-echoing around the room. Clutching at the shower curtain, she staggered backwards, ripping the curtain from its moorings. The end of the railing speared a mirror on the wall and it crashed down, too.

The door-handle rattled furiously, followed seconds later by a splintering sound as Nash burst into the room. 'What the hell...?'

Her parched throat refused to co-operate. 'There, in the bath,' she croaked, pointing frantically.

His sweeping gaze took in the pulsating body crouched in the tub, its presence multiplied horribly by the shards of mirror littered around it. 'It's all right, it's only a tarantula,' he said in a tone he might use to gentle a terrified animal.

'It's huge,' she gasped, turning her face away. 'How I hate spiders!'

'Phobia?' he queried gently. She nodded, biting on her lower lip to stop herself from screaming again. He took her arm and urged her towards him, keeping himself between her and the thing in the bath. 'Come on, I'll get you out of here.'

Fear held her frozen to the spot. 'I can't.'

'Yes, you can. Come to me, one step at a time, and mind the broken glass.'

Concentrating on the sound of his voice, and the reassuring grip of his fingers, she picked her way across the floor until she collapsed into his arms.

'It's all right, I've got you,' he said, sweeping her off her feet.

Seconds later she was deposited at the door of her room. He turned away and she grasped his arm. 'Where are you going?'

'To deal with the spider. I won't be long.'

True to his word, he strode back down the hall and she heard the sound of running water as he flushed the creature away. The image of it filled her mind and she shivered. He was at her side in an instant. 'Are you all right?'

'I will be. I wish I weren't such a coward.'

'Being afraid of something doesn't make you a coward,' he denied. 'A coward wouldn't confront a hooligan with a knife.'

She gave him a shaky smile. 'So how come I turn to jelly at the sight of a teensy spider?'

'You're tired and over-wrought or you probably wouldn't have reacted so badly. Besides, it wasn't so teeny. Seven inches across at least.'

A shudder rippled through her. 'And I thought everything was bigger in Texas. That thing looked as if it could eat a bird.'

'Some of them do,' he said without thinking. Seeing the horror on her face, he added, 'But most of them are harmless. Australian country people keep them around to catch flies.'

'Oh, lord.' She took a great gulp of air and at the same moment realised she was wearing nothing but the shower curtain. Blushing wasn't something she did very often but now she felt a slow burn start at her bare toes and work its way up her body until she was crimson from head to foot. Her fingers worked at the edge of the curtain. 'I'd better put something on.'

His dark gaze roved over her bare shoulders and neck, resting on the hand clutching the curtain against her breasts. The fabric rose and fell in time with her laboured breathing. 'You look lovely just as you are.'

The whispered compliment made the breath catch in her throat. Unnerved by the intimacy of the moment, she backed away from him into her room. His eyes stayed on her as he followed her and closed the door.

Only the bedside light was on, casting a pool of yellow light across the pillow. She had turned the bed down before going to the shower and there was an air of invitation about it. The rest of the room was in shadow.

The darkness turned Nash's eyes into shadowy pools and made his face seem more angular and devilish than ever. She trembled as he came closer, enveloping her in his arms in one smooth, irresistible motion.

Melting against him seemed like the most natural action in the world. Her body felt fluid, shaping itself to him as if she was liquid bronze, to be cast to his mould. The top buttons of his shirt were open and his dark chest hair teased her skin. She burrowed against him and heard his soft moan of response.

Tilting her head back, she stared upwards, her uncertain gaze seeking reassurance in the dark depths of his eyes, but they were hooded and unreadable. Tremors swept through her as his mouth travelled across her hot forehead and down her face where he continued to blaze a trail of kisses all the way to her lips. There he paused, drinking in her sweetness as if it was the breath of life itself.

'Oh, Nash,' she moaned, her lips moving against his. Parting even to speak seemed unthinkable.

'Beautiful, beautiful Jake.' The way he said her name, as if it was a caress, played havoc with her senses. Her panic over the spider seemed like calm reason compared to the torrent of sensations convulsing her now. She slid her hands down his back, exploring the ridges of his spinal column, wanting to know every inch of him as intimately as she knew her own body.

His rising passion inflamed her, too, until her thoughts spun wildly out of all control. She longed to feel his ruggedly masculine body possessing her, commanding her, bending her to his desires. For they were her desires, too. It was as if she had become a traveller embarking on a wondrous journey. She knew instinctively that they must go together, or not at all.

'Jake, this is wrong,' he growled. The admission was so startling that a denial leapt from her throat before she had time to think about it.

He pressed a finger to her lips. 'No, listen to me. I must leave you now, before it's too late.'

For her, it was already too late, had been so from the moment he followed her into the room, his eyes blazing with intimate messages.

'What is it? What have I done?' she asked, her mind refusing to accept that he meant to leave her alone despite the promise of his caresses.

His hands moved to her shoulders and he held her a little apart from him, resisting her instinctive attempt to press closer to him. 'You haven't done anything. I have to go, that's all.'

'If it's what you want to do.' Her voice was bleak with disappointment.

He swung away from her, the muscles of his broad shoulders bunching as he clenched and unclenched his hands at his sides. 'It isn't what I want at all, but it's . . . necessary.' He ground out the last word as if it was an oath.

Necessary for whom? She wrapped her arms around herself in a defensive gesture. Her responses must have betrayed her love for him, alerting his self-protective instincts. Why else would he shy away when she had felt for herself the strength of his need for her? Passion wasn't something you turned on and off like a tap. But he had, because he had sensed that she wanted more than he was prepared to give.

'Damn you, Nash Campbell,' she said, fighting the tears which threatened to engulf her. Shedding tears for him was a luxury when she needed them all for herself.

'It's no more than I deserve,' he said grimly. Handing her the robe he had retrieved from the bathroom, he waited until she had put it on then moved to the door. 'I have something to tell you.'

'What is it?' she asked disinterestedly.

'When I got back to my room, Chris had left a message to say that my mother is due back in Seymour tomorrow. I'm meeting her at the bus station and driving her home to Wirrinda.'

Still aching with the shock of rejection, Jake absorbed this new blow as if it was directed at someone else. 'Maybe she won't recognise me,' she said dully.

'I did,' he reminded her.

The agreement he had extracted from her hovered over her like a dark cloud. 'Then it's over,' she said. 'I'll stay here until I find another host family, or arrange to go back to Texas.'

He nodded, his face an expressionless mask. 'It would be for the best.'

Sadness settled over her like a leaden mantle. He wasn't even going to try to keep her around. Telling herself that it was no more than she had agreed didn't help. At the prospect of never seeing him again, she felt as if her world had come to an end.

When he left without another word, she went to the window and looked out, but the Southern Cross was blanketed by cloud, making navigation by the stars impossible. It seemed oddly appropriate. Would she ever find her way home again?

CHAPTER NINE

BY THE time Jake came down to breakfast next morning, Nash was gone and a sense of loss engulfed her as she passed the open door of his empty room. Would he have left if they *had* made love last night? There was no denying the intensity of his desire, yet he had pushed her away. Now she would never convince him that the ties of love weren't the shackles he believed they were.

For breakfast, she choked down some toast and orange juice, her usual hearty appetite deserting her. Afterwards, she walked to the nearby office of the local newspaper, the *Seymour Star*, which had been in existence for fifty years. They kept a complete file of all their back issues and the receptionist showed no surprise when she asked to see the papers from her birth year.

'Lots of people around here are doing family histories,' the receptionist informed her. 'But you're our first American.' He plonked a dusty book held together with metal clips on to the counter in front of her.

She stifled a sneeze as the dust rose in a cloud. 'My mother visited this district before I was born. I want to see if she's mentioned,' she explained.

'Oh, I see.' As she'd hoped, the ordinariness of her request stifled his interest and he left her alone with the files.

Thirty-seven issues of the *Seymour Star* later, she knew a great deal about life in the town during the year she was born, but nothing new about her family situation. Not surprisingly, she wasn't mentioned in the births, deaths and marriage announcements, although the social pages contained a single paragraph about a visit by Mr and Mrs Lyndon McVey of America to the district. Mrs McVey was visiting a childhood friend, Mrs Tom Campbell of Wirrinda. The Campbells were newcomers to the district and had purchased Wirrinda from the Foster-Gortons who had lived in the area since the 1800s, the report said.

The mention of the previous owners confirmed Nash's observation that they had taken years to be accepted by the local residents. Things would be very different now, she thought. There was no doubt that Wirrinda had prospered in Campbell hands.

Nash would be at the bus station by now, waiting for his mother to arrive, the Mrs Tom Campbell mentioned in the story. Thinking of them saddened Jake afresh. Then her mouth twisted into an ironic smile. Worrying that Susan Rand was her rival, she hadn't allowed for another woman's coming between them, his mother, Alice Campbell.

As she turned pages desultorily, her attention was drawn to a story which took up most of a front page. There was a photograph of a small car lying crushed beneath a bus. 'Local girl dies in tour mishap' was the headline. Jake might have overlooked the story if not for a reference to the owner of the car the girl was driving. It was Alice Campbell.

The driver had been Lynne Jamieson, a jillaroo at Wirrinda, who had borrowed the car with Mrs Campbell's permission to go to Seymour. The drive had ended in tragedy when the brakes of a tour bus had failed and it had ploughed headlong into the small car.

Jake's pulses quickened. The report added that Lynne Jamieson was the mother of a baby daughter who was being cared for at Wirrinda. American visitors, Mamie and Lyndon McVey, had offered to adopt the child if no other family could be found. A picture showed the McVeys holding the baby and looking sombrely into the camera.

At the sight of it, Jake's chest tightened. The photo was in the family album at home. She had never suspected that it had been taken half a world away, before the McVeys became her parents.

Wet drops splashed on to the page and she realised she was crying for the poor woman who lay crushed beneath the bus. Instinctively she knew it was her mother. Any hope that they would ever meet had been extinguished in the senseless tragedy.

Hungrily she devoured the small inset photo of Lynne Jamieson. She had been pretty but what had she been like as a person? Jake would never know.

A question began to gnaw at her. If Lynne Jamieson was her real mother, why was only one child mentioned? With an inner certainty, she knew that Chris was her sister, yet there was no record of her birth, and now no mention of her in the story. Jake's head began to ache with the effort of puzzling it out.

Stepping out into dazzling sunlight, she realised that the ache inside her was also hunger. She had eaten almost nothing for breakfast and it was already past midday. A café across the street looked inviting and she headed towards it.

'Need some company?'

'Hi, Susan. I was just going for coffee and a sandwich.' She tried to sound cordial as Susan Rand fell into step beside her but she had been hoping for some time alone with her thoughts.

'Then I'll join you for dinner. Or lunch, I should say,' Susan said, oblivious to Jake's introspective mood.

The café, called Checkers, was aptly named. It was divided into high-backed booths, with red gingham curtains and tablecloths giving it a cheerful air. Jake slid into a booth and Susan took the seat opposite her. Their order of toasted cheese sandwiches, french fries and coffee was soon in front of them.

Jake picked up a chip with her fingers and popped it into her mouth, finding some of her appetite returning. 'What keeps you in Seymour?' she asked Susan.

'Scott has some business to do before we drive back to Kookaburrah this afternoon.'

'I get the impression that Scott likes you,' Jake said, helping herself to a sandwich.

Susan dropped some artificial sweetener into her coffee. 'Seems foolish, using low-cal sweetener and eating french fries at the same time,' she said, seeming not to have heard Jake's comment. Then she grinned sheepishly. 'I kind of like Scott, too. He seemed too quiet at first, but he's really sweet when you get to know him.'

'I found him pleasant enough last night.'

Susan shot her an anxious look. 'It's all right, isn't it? I mean me bein' interested in Scott?'

'I thought you were sweet on Nash,' Jake said, her spirits lifting at the news.

The other girl twisted a paper napkin between her fingers. 'I like Nash, but Scott is special. You two were getting along so well last night that I thought I didn't stand a chance.'

'So you tried to make him jealous by flirting with Nash?'

Susan squirmed uncomfortably. 'It wasn't very kind, but it sure worked. After you two left, we got on famously.'

'I like Scott, but only as a friend,' Jake assured her. 'I'm glad you had a good time.'

'You-all didn't do so badly,' Susan said. 'At least Scott and I stayed in public. Rushing off pretending you were ill to make Nash follow you upstairs was inspired.'

'I didn't do it so he'd follow me,' Jake protested, but Susan remained unconvinced. Jake sighed. 'What does it matter, anyway? I won't be seeing Nash again.'

A sympathetic look crossed Susan's face and she reached for Jake's hand. 'Oh, honey, what happened?'

'Nothing. He was kind enough to fill in as my host after Bill Casey collapsed. But it was only temporary and I can't stay there any longer.'

'What will you do?'

Jake's shoulders lifted in an expressive shrug. 'I'm due for some time off. I may do a little sight-seeing then go home.'

'To Texas?'

'It's the only home I've got.' Jake sipped her coffee pensively. Johnny would be pleased. His letters made it clear that he still considered the McVey ranch to be half hers, although she had relinquished her right to it before leaving Texas. Putting it in writing didn't make it official, John said. She wondered if he had kept his vow to tear up the document as soon as she left.

Even if she went back now, it wouldn't be the same, she acknowledged. Riding the rolling green hills of the ranch, she would see in her mind's eye the eucalyptus forests and emerald waterways of the Riverina. She would watch for silver-grey kangaroos springing along the roadside, and listen for the musical call of the currawong, because this was her home now, too. Jean Crawford was right. Roots ran deeper than one imagined, exerting a pull when you least expected it.

Besides, a much stronger tie bound her to Australia, a tie of love. Despite Nash's insistence that love enslaved those who succumbed to it, she knew it brought its own kind of freedom—to know another person as well as you knew yourself, to share your deepest fears and dreams. Freedom from fear and loneliness were among its blessings.

But those blessings only came when your love was returned. A vision of a tall, broad-shouldered Aussie in a sway-brimmed bush hat filled her mind. As long as she loved him, she would never be free even if the whole Pacific Ocean separated them.

'Your coffee's getting cold,' Susan said, interrupting her reverie. The other woman slid out of the booth. 'While you finish it, I'll go to the ladies' room and do something with this sun-ravaged face of mine.'

Jake nodded absently, caught up in her thoughts. Moments later, she came fully alert with the arrival of two young men dressed in torn jeans, open-necked shirts and black leather jackets. The shorter of the two men was the rustler who had stabbed Nash.

Keeping her hand over her mouth to hide her face, she studied him as he joked with his companion about where they would sit. The police had taken possession of her photograph as evidence, but his face illuminated in the glare of the flash was burned into her memory.

She pretended to study the menu as they sauntered past and took a booth directly behind her. Jake heard them order milk shakes and hamburgers while making lewd comments which the waitress ignored.

'See, no one's recognised me,' one of the men said. Jake guessed that he was the rustler.

'All the same, Kev, you're taking a chance coming into town like this. I thought you were going to lie low at the shack until they stopped looking for you.'

'They won't stop,' the man called Kev growled. 'Not while they have my mug-shot up on the cop shop wall.'

'It's not very clear,' the other man said. 'I got a look at it when I went in for my bike registration. It's not enough to pin anything on you. If you lie low, they'll forget about you in no time.'

The man, Kev, gave a derisive snort. 'What makes you think I want them to forget about me? That farmer made a fool of me. I had a customer for those deer. Leaving them behind cost me plenty.'

They were interrupted when the waitress served their drinks and hamburgers. Jake waited impatiently, praying that Susan wouldn't come back until she had heard more. Knowing Susan, she was probably removing her entire make-up and reapplying it. With luck, she would be gone for ages.

Her thoughts were racing. If the men were right and the photograph wasn't a good enough likeness to convict them, what she learned might make a difference.

'You said you had a buyer for the deer,' the younger man said around a mouthful of food. 'I thought the whole thing was a lark, for the Leather Lions.'

'I put it about that it was a club initiation so that Ned and Davo would do the dirty work. You don't think they'd go along if I told them they were cattle duffers, do you?'

'You're something else,' the younger man said admiringly. 'I bet you weren't planning to split the profits, neither.'

There was a bubbling sound as Kev drank the dregs of his milk shake. 'I'm a businessman. What do you think?'

His companion chuckled. 'What will you do now? You can't risk having another go at those deer.'

'Why not? Who'd expect me to come back to the scene of the crime?' Their voices dropped and Jake had to strain to catch what they were saying. 'I'm going to need help and I can't ask Ned and Davo again, after what happened last time.'

'But I'm already in the Lions gang. I don't want to be initiated into no club.'

'How about the millionaire's club? There's big bucks to be made in this racket. Get it? Big bucks?'

Their laughter echoed around the booth and Jake waited tensely. She ached to confront them and demand to know their plans so she could forewarn Nash. The senseless laughter seemed to go on forever.

'Won't they be on the look-out for us?' the younger man asked, sobering abruptly.

She imagined Kev's answering nod. 'I hope they are. I'd like a chance to slice up that bastard, Campbell, only real good this time. If it wasn't for his interference, I'd be in the money by now. Besides,' he lowered his voice, 'I kinda liked the colour of his blood.'

Cold shivers swept through Jake. These men sounded as if they enjoyed hurting people. The pleasure in Kev's voice as he contemplated using his knife on Nash chilled her to the core. This was no teenage prank. Kev was using teenagers to do his dirty work. Somehow she had to warn Nash without letting these two know that she was on to them.

She consulted her watch. The meeting with Nash's mother would be over by now. Even if she caught up with him, it would look as if she was scheming to meet his mother for her own benefit. He might not even believe her story. And she couldn't call Chris without explaining why she wasn't coming back. What on earth was she to do?

There was a chorus of whistles and cat-calls as Susan made her way back to the booth. They subsided as she slid into the seat opposite Jake. 'Did you hear that?' She tossed her head in the direction of the men. 'Let's get out of here. Those two look like trouble.'

Jake was only too glad to oblige. Besides, she had an idea. 'Would Scott mind giving me a ride back to Wirrinda? I need to collect some things I left behind,' she improvised to allay Susan's curiosity.

'I'll ask Scott but I'm sure it's no problem.'

Jake remained in the booth while Susan paid their bill to the accompaniment of more cat-calls from the youths. They were too busy watching her to notice Jake slipping out of the café. By the time Susan joined her, Scott had pulled up in his car. It was unlikely that the man called Kev had seen much of her face behind the blinding camera flash, but she felt relieved to be in Scott's car and on her way to Wirrinda.

He was pleased to see her and accepted Susan's explanation that Jake had some things to collect before she moved on. 'Where are you going next?' he asked conversationally.

'Jake wants to see more of Australia before going home,' Susan put in for her.

Jake silently blessed her for the comment. It led to a pleasant discussion about the best places to see in Australia. The two-hour journey passed quickly, with no more awkward questions being asked. During the journey she kept a look-out for Nash's car. When she didn't see it, she assumed that he had taken his mother to lunch in Seymour before setting off for home.

'Are you sure you don't want me to drop you at the homestead?' Scott queried when she asked to be dropped off at the main road.

'No, thanks. I'll enjoy the walk.' The truth was, she didn't want to run into Chris at the homestead and have to explain why she hadn't travelled back with Nash. Her plan was to tell Len Crawford what she had learned. He would know what to do.

It took her half an hour to walk from the main road to the homestead. By the time she reached it, perspiration beaded her forehead and she could feel the sun burning her skin. Foolishly, she'd left her hat at the hotel. But when she left her room this morning, hiking back to Wirrinda was the last thing she expected to be doing.

The lawn-mower sound of a light plane shattered the bush stillness. Shading her eyes, she saw an old Tiger Moth heading north, away from the homestead. It was Chris's beloved Victor Victor. Chris was unlikely to spot her from this angle but just in case, Jake shrank against the bushes at the roadside until the plane was a speck on the horizon.

When she reached the homestead it was deserted, then Jean Crawford emerged from the main house carrying an overflowing basket of laundry. Seeing Jake, she broke into a smile which turned into a frown of puzzlement when she looked around and saw no car. 'Where's Nash? I thought he was bringing Alice back with you.'

'He is, but not until later. I hitched a ride with Scott Howard.'

'Surely he didn't leave you at the gate? It's a long walk on such a hot day.'

'It was my idea. I didn't realise how far it was.' Jake kept her tone conversational, but inside she was burning with impatience. She endured a few more pleasantries before she was able to ask, 'Where will I find Len?'

In the midst of hanging out the clothes, Jean paused. 'They're cutting a firebreak along the back paddocks today. Is anything the matter?'

Concealing her disappointment, Jake shook her head. Why couldn't Len have been working closer to home today, of all days? The back paddocks were a long drive away over roads she hadn't yet travelled. Firebreaks were cut using bulldozers and graders, so the men were out of touch for some time. 'Did he say when he'd be coming back?' she asked.

Jean brightened. 'That I do know. He has to be here by four to take an important phone call. Shall I tell him you want to see him?'

By four, the rustlers could have cleared out the chital paddock. 'I'll leave a note, telling him where I'll be,' she volunteered.

'I can give him a message when he gets back,' Jean offered, but Jake was already out of earshot. She had wasted too much time already.

Sketching out the details of Kev's plans, she pinned the folded note to the station notice-board, where Nash and Len would see it when they returned. Checking the board was routine for everyone so there was no chance that her note would be missed. She only hoped that they would act quickly when they read it.

In daylight, driving to the chital paddock was much easier than covering the same distance by night. She was just congratulating herself on making good time when there was a loud report and the vehicle slewed across the road. 'Oh, no, not a puncture now,' she moaned, slamming her hands against the steering wheel in frustration. The limp nearside tyre told its own story. For a few seconds the air turned blue with some colourful Australian epithets she'd learned from the men, but then she got herself under control and set about changing the wretched tyre.

Thanks to the puncture, the light was fading by the time she reached her destination. There was no sign of Kev or his accomplice as she cut her engine and glided the last few feet. Nosing the car into a clump of bushes, she crept up to the paddock on foot.

The deer seemed to sense that something was amiss. Instead of grazing peacefully, they stood bunched together, heads up and pointed ears straining. The scattering of white dots on each animal looked luminous in the setting sun.

She was upwind of the herd so they weren't scenting her presence. Kev and the other man must be nearby. Her nerves were stretched to near breaking point. Where were they?

Then she spotted their vehicle, a battered utility truck in which they must intend to transport the stolen deer. She wasn't fooled by the vehicle's rough appearance. In it, the rustlers had outrun Len and his men once already. A closer inspection revealed twin chrome exhausts camouflaged with mud. What other modifications had they made to ensure a speedy getaway?

The crack of a rifle shot brought her head up and a chill engulfed her as one of the chital hinds tumbled over. Another crack and another deer went down. She had to do something before Nash lost the entire herd.

There was a shotgun in Nash's car but it was unloaded for safe travelling. Nervousness made her fumble the simple task of loading the weapon and she cursed her clumsiness. Before she could finish, a voice challenged her. 'What do you think you're doing, lady?' She froze as the unmistakable bulk of a rifle muzzle was jammed against her spine.

Kev reached around and lifted the shotgun from her hands. 'Good girl. Now turn around and let me look at you.'

Letting the cartridges drop, unnoticed, into the long grass, she turned. The malevolence in his face filled her with horror. Close-up, he was no teenager. He was a man, cursed with a boy's scrawny build and height. It probably explained his antisocial behaviour.

'What are you going to do with me?' she asked, thinking how inane the question sounded. Did she really want to know?

'We might treat you the same as them deer,' he leered. 'How'd you like that, Miss America?'

'You can't mean to shoot me?' In spite of herself, her voice shook with fear. He looked perfectly capable of gunning her down in cold blood.

'Kev, what's the hold-up?' The other man emerged from the bushes and paled at the tableau confronting him. 'Bloody hell! What's she doing here?'

'Spying on us for Campbell. There's some rope in the ute. Get it for me, will you?'

If he meant to tie her up, he wasn't going to shoot her, she thought, relief making her knees go weak. But the feeling was short-lived. 'We're going to have some fun with Miss America.'

The other man spun around. 'Now wait a minute. This isn't cattle duffing. I didn't plan on anything like this.'

'Then you can watch. I don't care. Just get the bloody rope.'

With obvious reluctance, the other man disappeared into the bushes where she had spotted their car. There was a scuffling sound and Kev yelled over his shoulder, 'You all right, Mick?'

'No, he isn't all right,' came a ringing voice. 'He's under arrest. You're on your own.'

Nash emerged from the bushes and faced Kev, a rifle held loosely across his body. There was menace in every line of his stance. His eyes were black with fury and muscles worked in his jaw, as if he was controlling himself with an effort of will.

Kev took a step back, obviously intimidated by the sight, but not enough to concede defeat. 'You want me, come and get me,' he said.

'Let the girl go and you can walk out of here,' Nash stated. The coldness in his voice sent shivers up Jake's spine. She had never seen him look so terrifying. Yet he managed to send messages of reassurance to her in waves, as if his thoughts were reaching out to her. She gave a tiny nod and he looked momentarily startled, as if he hadn't expected her to receive his thought-messages. Then his eyes became cold again. 'I said let her go.'

'An' if I don't?'

'You'll wish you'd never been born.' He let the threat sink in, then added, 'What kind of spider are you, anyway?'

The rustler looked puzzled and Jake frowned, too. The insult sounded odd even to her Texan ears. Then she understood. Nash was sending her a message.

Conjuring up an image of the tarantula in the hotel bathroom, she filled her lungs with air and screamed loudly enough to startle a flock of cockatoos into flight from a nearby tree. She kept on screaming until her throat was raw and her lungs threatened to burst.

Kev looked stunned. 'Bloody hell!' Then he backed away. 'I never touched her, I never.'

By the time he realised it was a diversion, Len and his men had pinned him from behind and wrestled the weapons away from him. He put up no more resistance as he was led away.

The last of her screams echoed on the air and she leaned against the car, fighting for breath. In seconds, Nash was beside her, his rifle discarded as he crushed her to him. His kisses covered her hair and face. Hungrily, she kissed him back, deliriously happy to be alive and in his arms once more.

Holding her at arm's length, he inspected her worriedly. 'He didn't harm you in any way?'

'No, he didn't, thanks to you. But he shot the deer.' Her voice rose with alarm as she remembered the awful scene.

The pressure of his hands tightened against her back. 'It was only with a tranquilliser gun. They'll recover completely as soon as they receive the antidote, and my men are taking care of it now.'

'And Kev? What will happen to him?'

'The law will deal with him. He's using the local bikie gang as a cover, recruiting teenagers to steal stock for him, so he's probably wanted for a string of offences. You were crazy to tackle him on your own.'

The censure in his voice brought tears to her eyes until she saw that his anger masked his concern for her. 'I didn't know what else to do,' she said.

'Except try and get yourself killed. You're a fool, Jake McVey, a beautiful, headstrong, desirable fool.'

'I'm not,' she protested.

'Which?' he teased.

'A headstrong fool,' she said weakly.

His eyes glowed as he looked down at her. 'But you *are* beautiful and desirable. Dear heaven, Jake, why do you keep doing this to me?'

Since she didn't know what it was she did, she couldn't answer and in any case, her head was buzzing and tears blurred her vision. Nash seemed to be a long way away from her. 'I think I'm going to pass out,' she murmured as she felt herself start to fall.

'No, you aren't, you're going to hold on until we reach the homestead,' he said decisively.

She fought off the engulfing darkness. 'You can't take me there. Your mother——'

'Knows you're here,' he interrupted. 'Oh, not who you are, but that we have an American trainee called Jake. My mother is asleep right now so it's quite safe.'

Disappointment welled inside her. Nothing had changed, at least not where she was concerned.

In a half-conscious stupor brought on by exhaustion and shock, she endured the drive back to the homestead. She was barely conscious of being lifted out of the car and carried to a bedroom where she sank on to soft pillows with a murmur of gratitude.

'Not so fast. You're covered in mud,' Nash told her.

Some of her torpor vanished as he unzipped her jeans and slid them down her legs, the cool air wafting across her skin. 'I can do it,' she protested feebly.

Ignoring her protestations, he proceeded to undress her with economical movements. She was fully awake now and aware of his quickened breathing and he gave her a thorough sponge bath where she lay. Now and then he muttered angrily over the bruises she had collected in the scuffle.

One of the bruises was painful and she moaned when he touched it. 'Poor baby,' he murmured, leaning over her. 'I'll kiss it better.'

The effect of the kiss was electrifying. She cupped her hands to his head, drawing his mouth down to hers. The sponge dropped to the floor as he gathered her into his arms.

Dizziness washed over her again, but this time he was the cause. His mouth was so demanding that her lips felt bruised by the pressure. They parted softly and a wave of heat rushed through her as his tongue did a seductive dance around her mouth.

As the slow, languorous kiss deepened, his hands slid along her body, sending sparks of electric feeling along every inch of her. When his fingers glided between silk and skin, her breath came in shallow gasps. Down and down his touch strayed until she arched against him in ecstasy. Flames leapt along her veins, threatening to consume her before she could know the sweetness of his ultimate possession.

Could one die of sensory overload? It seemed all too possible as his hands returned to her breasts, his touch tormentingly sweet as he pushed aside the lace fabric of her bra.

A sharp moan made her open her eyes and she was shocked to see the blackness in his expression. He looked like a soul in torment, his eyes blazing as much with pain as with passion. 'What is it, Nash?' she asked. What could make him look so driven?

'This. What we're doing.' Even as he forced the words out, his mouth sought hers and his hands glided feather-light over the curve of her hip. 'You should send me away.'

The answer was ragged but heartfelt. 'But I don't want you to go. I want you to love me, Nash.'

'And I do,' he ground out. 'Dear heaven, I tried not to, but you're a fever in my blood and there's only one cure.'

Like a man possessed, he straightened and shed his clothes, casting them heedlessly to right and left. When he came to her, the loving was as perfect as she had dreamed it would be.

But when she opened her eyes to gaze lovingly at him, to tell him that everything was all right, she was chilled by the bleakness in his expression. He looked like a man who hated himself for what he had just done.

CHAPTER TEN

SUNLIGHT spilling across her face roused Jake from a deep sleep. A smile curved the corners of her mouth upwards. She had been dreaming that she and Nash had made love.

Warmth flooded through her. The dream had been so vivid that she shivered with remembered pleasure just thinking about it. She stretched languorously, then her eyelids snapped open and she sat up. It was no dream. She was back in her room at Wirrinda and Nash *had* made love to her last night.

Memories crowded in thick and fast. The encounter with the rustlers at the chital paddock. Nash saving her from Kev and his accomplice. Undressing and bathing her. It was all vividly clear and heat suffused her face as she recalled what had happened next.

From caring and gentle, his ministrations had changed to sensual and demanding until she hadn't been able to subdue the tidal wave of response which had curled over her. In turn, she had ignited his desire until it burned like a roman candle, incandescent in its intensity, beyond any man's power to resist.

If he could have resisted it, she was certain that he would have done. The look of horror on his face afterwards told her so. His eyes had blazed, but with self-loathing, as if he hated himself for what he was doing, yet couldn't hold himself back.

A shudder shook her and she hugged the covers up to her chin. Why should he hate himself when their union had felt so idyllic? She wasn't ashamed of loving him, but he seemed to regret his part. It made no sense at all.

There was a knock on the door and Chris poked her head around it. 'Good morning, sleepyhead.'

Jake managed to smile. 'Howdy, Chris. Did I oversleep?'

The other girl grinned. 'By a couple of hours, but by all accounts you earned the right. When I got back yesterday, Len told me what you did.' She nudged the door with her shoulder and came in carrying a laden tray. 'Nash told me to let you sleep as long as you liked. Breakfast in bed was my special touch.'

'There's no need to pamper me,' she insisted. 'I'm fine, really.'

'But you had a rough experience, and you did save the chital herd.'

Jake frowned. 'Thinking about it now, it was a crazy thing to do. I should have called the police and let them handle it.'

'Until a crime was actually committed, they probably couldn't have intervened anyway.'

'All the same, Nash and Len are the real heroes,' Jake insisted. 'If they hadn't turned up, I shudder to think what could have happened.'

'Well, it didn't, and the farmers around here should be grateful to you. It seems as if Kev Riley was the head of a substantial stock stealing ring which the police can now close down. So relax and enjoy being a heroine while it lasts.'

All the same, she felt uncomfortable allowing Chris to place the tray across her knees and pour steaming coffee into her cup. 'Where is Nash this morning?' she asked. She had slept so deeply that she hadn't heard him return to his own room during the night.

'He went off early to cut firewood.' Chris opened the curtains wide and sunlight flooded into the room.

'And your mother?' Jake asked carefully.

'She was exhausted after her journey yesterday. I suggested that she spend the day in bed.'

Which was probably why Nash felt safe leaving her alone at the homestead. He knew there was no chance she could run into his mother and ask awkward questions. A chill settled over her, despite the warmth of the morning. She reached a sudden decision. 'Did Nash mention that I'm leaving today?'

Chris looked surprised. 'No, he didn't. Aren't you happy here, Jake?'

She was happier here than she had ever been anywhere, but she couldn't tell Chris the reason why she still had to go. 'I'm not unhappy. But the Agricultural Association isn't keen to have a single man acting as host to a female trainee.'

'So your stay was temporary from the beginning?'

Jake nodded. 'I'm afraid so. But I'm sure my new host family will be wonderful. I may not be billeted too far away.'

'I hope not. It's been lovely having you here, Jake. You're like one of the family.'

More than she could possibly know, Jake thought miserably, and sipped the coffee to hide her troubled expression. 'I've enjoyed my stay, too,' she assured Chris. It wasn't fair to let her sister think otherwise when she had done so much to make Jake feel at home. 'I'm going to miss you,' she added, not realising that she had voiced the thought until Chris nodded.

'Me, too.' Then she brightened. 'But you can't leave yet, no matter what the Association says. You're needed as a witness by the police.'

'But I wasn't the only one who saw the rustlers,' she protested. 'Len and Nash caught them red-handed.'

'Mmm, you have a point. Maybe they want to compare your stories to give them a stronger case.'

'If they only want a statement——'

'They can come and interview you here,' Chris decided. Jake had started to suggest going to the police station in Seymour, but if she insisted Chris was bound to wonder why she was so anxious to get away. It seemed as if she was stuck at Wirrinda for the time being.

Despite Chris's insistence that she stay in bed, Jake showered and dressed in jeans and a fringed western shirt, hoping that the bright colours would lift her mood. Then she made her way to the kitchen. Accustomed to being active, she couldn't sit around when there was nothing the matter with her.

It wasn't strictly true, she thought as she got out the ingredients to make bread. Her shower had revealed some nasty bruises from her encounter with the rustlers. There was also an ache inside her which had nothing to do with her adventure. It came from facing the fact that Nash might want her in his bed, but there was no place for her in his life.

Several times, he had almost made love to her but had ruled his passions with the force of his will. Last night, passion had won out over reason and he hated himself for it. The last thing he wanted was a permanent attachment and he thought she expected it after last night. How else could she explain the reproach she had seen in his eyes when he looked at her?

Taking out her frustration on the bread dough helped. Thumping it around not only worked off her bad feelings but made the dough lighter. She had never been able to work out the reason. Maybe it was nature's safety valve. She covered the fragrant mass with a damp tea towel and set it in a warm corner of the kitchen to rise.

Her back was turned to the kitchen door and she was elbow-deep in soapy water, when the door opened behind her. 'Chris, have you seen...?'

At the sound of Nash's voice, every nerve-ending sprang to vibrant life. She kept her back turned. 'Chris got a phone-call after breakfast. Her flying doctor is in the area and she's gone to meet him in Victor Victor. Can I help you with anything?'

'I doubt it.' His tone was sharp and cold. He was still angry about last night.

She swathed her hands in a towel and spun around. 'Don't you think you should tell me why you're so angry? If it concerns me, I have a right to know.'

'It doesn't concern you,' he snapped. 'One night in bed with me doesn't give you any rights at all.'

He stormed out of the kitchen, leaving her staring after him, wounded to the core. Tears shimmered in her eyes and she trembled with emotion. He made what they had shared sound cheap and casual, as if it had no right to matter to her. He must know that it wasn't like that for her. Maybe that was the problem. He was afraid she had read too much into it, and wanted to warn her off.

Well, she wasn't going to be treated this way. He was wrong if he thought she expected a lifetime's commitment from him. She didn't want anything that he wasn't willing to give, but she was entitled to some basic consideration. Showing her a little respect wouldn't jeopardise his precious independence, would it?

Throwing the towel aside, she stalked out of the kitchen and looked around, wondering where he could have gone. Then she heard a commotion in the workshop. Someone was throwing tools around and cursing in a low voice. She followed the angry sounds.

She found him in the workshop with a chainsaw stretched across his knees as he worked with file and screwdriver to file burrs off the cutter bar. 'What happened to it?' she asked in a conversational tone, although the tangle of chain told its own story.

'I adjusted the chain and started her up without tightening the tension bolts,' he growled. 'Damned stupid machine. Chain's hopelessly tangled.'

Her mouth twitched as she heard him blaming the machine. It was an elementary mistake for someone who used a chainsaw as often as Nash did and she shook her head in wonder. What on earth was the matter with him?

She moved closer and surveyed his bent head. How she longed to run her fingers through his thick, dark hair. A dizzying current of desire raced through her and she throttled it off. Loving him had already created a mile-high barrier between them. She was only torturing herself needlessly by imagining such things.

He looked up and her heart gave a mad lurch. 'Was there something you wanted?'

Fighting the impulse to drop down beside him and bury her face in his lap, she lifted her head higher. 'I think you owe me an explanation.'

His mouth twisted into a sneer. 'I don't *owe* you a thing.' He avoided meeting her eyes and she wondered what dark thoughts hovered behind his hooded gaze.

She took a steadying breath. 'Very well, but human decency demands that you tell me what I've done wrong.' Her composure almost shattered and she cast an appealing look at him. 'Please, Nash, don't do this to me.'

'So you think what happened last night gives you a hold over me, do you?' he asked harshly.

'Of course not,' she denied. 'You've got it wrong. Love doesn't hold anyone. It sets you free, if you give it a chance.'

He gave all his attention to the chainsaw. 'Well I don't intend to give it a chance. You shouldn't have come here, Jake.'

'I can't leave until I know what I've done wrong,' she said, thinking that he meant she shouldn't have followed him to the workshop.

'I meant to Australia,' he said, contradicting her thoughts. 'If you'd stayed in Texas where you belong, none of this would have happened.'

She dropped to her knees beside him. 'You're wrong,' she said on an out-rush of breath. '*This* is where I belong and neither you, nor anyone, can send me away before I'm ready to go.'

The stony façade cracked at last and his dark eyes became moist. 'I was afraid of that. Dear heaven, what have I done?'

The gaze he turned to her was so filled with suffering that an answering ache resonated deep inside her. 'What we did wasn't wrong,' she denied, her voice cracking. But something in his expression alerted her. 'Was it, Nash?'

He set the chainsaw aside and rested his forearms on his knees. 'Oh, Jake, Jake. What happened between us is as wrong as it can possibly be. You see . . . oh, heavens, how do I tell you?' She waited, her heart racing as the silence lengthened. Finally, he said in a voice totally drained of emotion, 'I think you're my father's illegitimate child.'

As his words hammered into her brain, her voice rose on a wail of shock. 'Oh, no, no. It can't be.' She leapt to her feet and whirled away from him, coming up against the edge of the workbench. Flattening her palms against it, she turned to him. 'It can't be true. Lynne Jamieson was my mother. I read about her death in the *Seymour Star*.'

'I'm sorry,' he said with genuine compassion. 'I know what it must mean to you. But it doesn't change the fact that my father was her lover.'

Her throat ached with tears but she choked them back, afraid that if she cried now she wouldn't be able to stop. He couldn't be her half-brother. Her brain rejected the very idea. If he was, she couldn't love him, not in the way every fibre of her being wanted to love him. *Already* loved him, she acknowledged painfully. Nothing could change that, not even the shocking possibility which he was forcing her to consider. 'I can't believe it. I *won't* believe it,' she insisted, her head swinging from side to side. Her palms slammed against the workbench again and again until they were raw, but she couldn't stop.

'Jake, don't, please.' He moved to her side and his hands clamped around her wrists, stilling the hysterical movements. 'You mustn't torture yourself. I've done enough of that for both of us.'

Her eyes, huge with suffering, lifted to his face. 'Then you don't hate me after all?'

'How can I hate the woman I love more than life itself?' His smouldering gaze took in her pale face and travelled to the cleft between her breasts, where his head had rested only last night. His breathing became laboured and his grip on her wrists tightened. 'For years, I've resisted falling in love, and when I finally do, nature plays a cruel joke on me. Some justice, isn't it?' He shifted away, his muscular back turned to her.

'How can you be sure that Tom Campbell is my father?' she asked. His hopelessness had communicated itself to her and her tone was listless.

'After you told me you couldn't find any record of Chris's birth, I went looking for her birth certificate,' he said in an oddly flat voice. He sounded as if all emotion had died inside him and her heart ached for him. The massive shoulders moved slightly as he looked at her. 'The certificate I found had been altered in several places but the father's name was Tom Campbell. There's worse,' he said as she started to speak. 'I also found a love-letter from Lynne to my father.'

Her fingers whipped to her mouth to stifle a cry. 'If Lynne was Chris's natural mother and Tom Campbell was the father...'

'Then they're your parents, too,' he stated.

'If you're right and we *are* twins.'

His searching gaze raked her face. 'Have you any real doubts?'

'No.' If she had, they had been dispelled the moment she'd met Chris Campbell. From the first, she had sensed an almost psychic bond between them which went beyond liking or friendship. She couldn't explain how she was so certain. She just felt that they had shared much more in life than friends could. It was the same certainty which members of the same family felt when they met after a lifetime of separation. Such bonds were undeniable. Chris felt it, too, she was positive.

He saw the acceptance in her eyes. 'It adds up, doesn't it? If my father had an affair with Lynne Jamieson, they would have concocted the adoption story to prevent a scandal.'

Her mind reeled. 'But why would they let you think that Chris was adopted if she was your father's natural child?'

He spread his hands wide, palms upwards. 'So I would do exactly what I did, keep quiet about what I'd learned for all these years. I didn't ask any awkward questions which might have uncovered the truth.'

'And they didn't want Chris to know, not because she was adopted, but because she wasn't. It was all a convenient fiction to hush up a scandal.' A new horror dawned on Jake. 'But if he was my real father, they gave away his natural child. How could they do such a thing?'

'I don't believe it's as terrible as it sounds.' The calmly reasoned way he said it suggested that he had given the matter a lot of thought. 'You've heard of surrogate parents?' She nodded and he went on, 'I think that's what my parents did for Mamie McVey. Could she bear her own children?'

'Not for years and years,' Jake said, remembering Mamie saying she had longed for a child but remained barren until Jake's arrival. 'They were married for eleven years before I was born. If you're right and your parents gave me to the McVeys, it must have seemed like a miracle to them. They treated me like fragile china.' She gave a choked laugh. 'I became a tomboy to prove that I couldn't be wrapped in cotton wool. My mother always hated my nickname.'

'Now you know why.'

She chewed on her lower lip in agonised thought. 'But it doesn't explain how they were able to have John. He was born on the ranch.'

'Once they had you, they probably stopped trying and nature did the rest. It's happened plenty of times.'

He was right. The newspapers were full of accounts of couples adopting a child as a last resort, then conceiving naturally when the pressure was off. It was starting to look as if he was right about everything.

Her face darkened with despair. If the man she thought of as her lover was truly her half-brother, how could she live with the fact? Could she ever look at him without wanting to feel his arms around her and his mouth on hers? He was fighting the same battle, she saw from the hard glitter which lit his gaze and the way he clenched his fists at his sides.

'What are we going to do?' she whispered as misery welled up inside her.

A muscle jumped in his cheek. 'The only thing we can do. You'll go back to Texas and I'll stay here and we'll both go on living, somehow.'

Her body swayed as if his words carried a physical impact but she recognised the soundness of his logic. As long as they were together, they were in danger of succumbing to the forces which had claimed them last night. Fate had played the most cruel trick possible on them and all they could do was walk away.

Her hopelessness was mirrored in her question. 'Will I ever see you again?'

He took a step towards her then checked himself. 'This has to be the end, for everyone's sake.'

'No!' The denial was torn from her throat and before she knew what she was doing she had launched herself across the room at him. His arms went around her automatically and he crushed her against his chest so hard that the life was almost squeezed out of her. She made no sound, only objecting when he held her away from him. 'I know,' she said abjectly. 'I guess I just don't have the strength to walk out of here.'

'Then I'll do it for both of us.'

And he did, while she stood her ground, every nerve-ending in her body quivering with the need to run after him. She couldn't let him walk out of her life, never to see him again. Yet he was right. There was no other way. 'I love you,' she murmured softly, tears streaming from her eyes and blurring her last, precious sight of him.

'Then why are you letting him go?' queried a soft voice behind her.

Unmoving, she bowed her head. 'I have no choice. If we have the same father...'

'Dear lord, is that what you think?'

She spun around, gasping in dismay at the sight of the frail woman standing in the passageway which led back to the house.

Dressed in a shimmering silk dressing-gown and high-heeled slippers, she was stunningly beautiful for a woman Jake guessed to be in her mid-fifties. Her silver hair was coiled into a French knot on top of her head, and her skin was so finely translucent that it seemed to be made of paper. The likeness to Nash gave away her identity at once. 'Mrs Campbell.'

'So you're Jake,' the woman said softly. She held out her hands. 'Come here, let me look at you.'

Shock still gripped Jake, making everything seem slightly unreal. Dazedly, she took the woman's hands. They were so fine that Jake feared to grip them for fear of hurting her. 'How did you know?'

'That Jake wasn't a man? Mamie wrote and told me what you insisted on calling yourself. The moment Nash said your name, I knew my day of reckoning had finally come.'

'You heard everything?'

Alice Campbell inclined her head. 'Enough to see that you had worked it all out so cleverly.'

Jake's spirits plummeted. So it was true. Tom Campbell was her natural father, the confirmation ending any hope of a love between herself and Nash. 'What should I call you?' she asked, confused.

Alice Campbell gave a gentle smile. 'I hope you'll call me Mother, but first there are things you must know. Shall we have some tea? I know how you Texans love your iced tea.'

It seemed incongruous to be talking of tea when her life had just crashed to an end. But something about this lovely, frail woman calmed her troubled spirit. 'I'd like that,' she agreed and followed Alice back to the house.

Waving aside Jake's protestations, Alice made the tea herself. 'Mamie taught me how you like it,' she said, filling tall glasses with ice and adding lemon wedges. Then she poured tea into the glasses. 'I'm sorry it isn't sun tea,' she apologised.

Sun tea was literally left in the sun to warm. 'This is fine, thank you,' Jake said, accepting the drink. She held the glass to her forehead for a second to soothe her feverish skin. 'You must have known my mother...Mamie,' she amended, 'very well.'

Alice smiled. 'She couldn't tell you without giving too much of your background away, but Mamie and I were practically sisters. She and her father lived in our house when he was posted to Sydney by his firm. Tom Campbell was her penfriend so I have her to thank for introducing us.'

Jake knew that Mamie McVey had visited Australia but had no idea how much time she had spent there. 'You must have loved her very much,' she said huskily.

'To give her a child, you mean?' Alice's soft laugh tinkled between them. 'Tom and I did love her, but not enough to give her his flesh and blood.'

The colour drained from Jake's face. 'But you said I should call you Mother.'

'And I hope you will,' Alice said serenely, 'when you marry my son. You see,' she went on before Jake could speak, 'Tom and I did give Mamie a child, but it wasn't Tom's. Mamie and Lyndon were here when our jillaroo, Lynne Jamieson, gave birth to twin babies. She hid her pregnancy so well that no one knew until they were born. I acted as her midwife.'

'She died soon afterwards, didn't she?' Jake said. 'I read about the accident in the local newspaper.'

'Then you know how your parents adopted you?' Jake nodded. 'By a twist of fate, Lynne got the registration of the births mixed up. Instead of registering Jacqueline *and* Christine, as she intended, the clerk put down "Jacqueline Christine."'

Jake's eyes widened. 'No wonder I couldn't find any trace of Chris's records.'

'Her birth was never registered. When I found out what had happened, I decided it was God's will. You see, I had had a little girl only a short time before, but she died in her cot soon after birth.'

'So you altered her birth certificate and gave it to Chris, which is why you and Tom are shown as the parents.'

Alice passed a delicate hand over her eyes. 'I know it was wrong and I've lived with the knowledge for twenty-five years, hardly knowing a peaceful moment. Except when I look at my lovely daughter, then I know I was justified. Did I really do such a terrible thing?' In the next breath, she answered her own question. 'You're both well and happy, raised v

'But what a from Lynne?'

Alice look ove with Tom, poor g child had deserted her an neone desperately, so she convince Tom loved her. Nothing he could sa uade her. She died still clinging to l y.'

'My poor mother.'

'I know. I t be hard for you, but never forget that Mamie ey was your mother in every way which matte '

'I know. ed a little time.'

A shado arkened Alice's face. 'Funny, Tom said the sa thing when I begged him to let me keep Chris. e hated wrong-doing of any kind but he loved m nd I got my way. I fear that my decision trou d him so much that he lost concentration whe he was building the dam. Losing him was my ret ution.'

A figure omed in the doorway. Nash stood there and one lo k at his stony expression showed that he had hea d everything.

Alice reached out a trembling hand to him. 'Can you ever forgive me, son?'

His rapier glance impaled her. 'So many lies, so much heartache. You're asking a lot.'

'But she lost her child, your sister,' Jake appealed to him. 'Can't you see, the deception was for the best of reasons?'

A crack appeared in his icy facade as he turned to Jake. 'You can ask me to forgive her after what she did to you?'

'What did she do except give me a home and people who loved me?' She willed him to be gentle with his mother. She had already suffered so much for her actions. 'Nash, can't you see, she has also set us free?'

Alice rose smoothly, her silk gown rustling in the silence which descended suddenly. 'I'll leave you children alone,' she murmured. On her way out, her hand grazed Nash's arm and Jake held her breath, only releasing it when Nash's hand covered his mother's in silent communion. Alice's step was light as she left them alone.

Across the room, the brilliance of Nash's gaze made Jake catch her breath. 'I'm glad you've chosen to forgive her. Losing her own child must have temporarily disturbed her reason. At least now we know why she took your father's death so dreadfully hard. All these years, she's been blaming herself.'

'It was guilt which destroyed her, not love at all,' he said on a thoughtful note. 'Thank the lord I found out in time.' He took a step towards her then another and swept her up into his arms.

She felt giddy with happiness. Her eyes blazed with all the tenderness she had locked inside. At last she could set it free. Seeing her expression, he let out a great shout of laughter and his whole body shook with the joy of it. She ran her hands down his back, her fingers sensitive to every rippling muscle, while he kissed her over and over, hungry for the touch of her mouth as if he could never have enough of her.

Tongues of fire leapt inside her and she clung to him. Never again would they be parted for more than the shortest time. She would ride where he rode, share his nights and days, and all the tomorrows that were granted to them.

At the thought, a tiny flicker of uncertainty gnawed at her. Now that they were free to love, was he really promising so much? She gazed up at him, her eyes wide with the fears fluttering inside her like tiny moths.

He saw the look and held her tightly against him, raining kisses on to her face as if he would never stop. 'Do you think you can live without Texas?' he asked hoarsely.

Her love shone diamond-bright out of her eyes. 'More easily than I could live without you.'

'We'll be married here in the summer and have our honeymoon in Texas; that way you'll have the best of both worlds,' he promised her.

She linked her arms around his neck and burrowed her face against his chest, hearing his heart thump like a drumbeat against her cheek. 'I thought I already did.'

A plane purred overhead and they heard it turn towards the airstrip. Nash smiled at her. 'Chris is on her way home. We'll have a few surprises for her, won't we?'

Now that there was no reason to keep the truth from her, Jake looked forward to sharing the future with her twin. 'I always wanted a real sister,' she said radiantly.

He nuzzled the side of her neck, his breath warm and sensuous. 'I didn't,' he growled, 'not if it was going to be you.' He had carried her halfway to the bedroom when she realised where he was taking her.

'We can't. Chris will be back soon,' she protested laughingly.

His mouth fastened on hers, silencing her in the most erotic way. 'I have a hunch that Mum will want to talk to Chris first,' he said. 'The best thing we can do is keep out of their way.' She was in no doubt as to how to meant them to fill the time, and the idea made her dizzy with anticipation.

When Nash was in such an autocratic mood, there was no point in arguing with him. Besides, she reminded herself, as an incandescent glow erupted inside her, a good Texan wife never argued with her husband—at least about some things.